MANITOULIN MEMORIES

MANITOULIN MEMORIES

by W.J. Reeves

Introduction

Manitoulin Memories is a collection of coming of age stories set in Canada in the 1950s. They are about a man who's recalling his father and take place in Manitoulin Island, Ontario, Canada which is now dead, consumed by civilization. After WW II, tourists came to the island from the States for a summer getaway. Manitoulin Memories deals with those who came and what they found and how they ended up; it makes use of a middle-aged man who returns to the Manitoulin to see how it is and to learn who he was when he lived there.

Manitoulin Island is the largest freshwater island in the world which, as a fact, shrinks in significance the more you think about it. On a map, the Manitoulin is a blob of land dividing the southern half of Lake Huron from its North Channel.

About the Author

W.J. Reeves, a professor in Brooklyn, came east to get married and to work, but he never forgot the Manitoulin.

Acknowledgments

I would like to thank my wife, Cathie, for her support these many years. I would also like to thank Rebecca Swift for creating the cover and Karen Carter for editing the stories. Finally, I would like to thank 52Novels.com for preparing Manitoulin Memories for e-book publishing. I have a special thanks for Albert Zayat, author, for his sage advice.

Table of Contents

Dragging

On a day such as this, as a boy, the man had fished for men on Manitoulin Island, the largest freshwater island in the world.

Today, the Verrazano Bridge was a parking lot. Today, getting to Brooklyn would be a long time coming. Three lanes across, 100 cars deep, all the cars jammed with commuters stuck in mid-commute at the middle of the bridge.

The tall man left the comfort of his warm car. A northeast wind drove cold rain into his face. He looked down at the water, full of whitecaps, blowing into New York harbor, heading for the Lady of Liberty. The water ran deep here, at least 50 fathoms.

"Is there an accident?" said a voice by his side.

"No," said the man, adjusting his Kohl binoculars.

"How can those help you see ahead?"

"I'm not looking ahead."

"Where're you looking?"

"Up."

"Up?"

"Yeah, up," said the man, pointing with his right hand at the supports that ran to the top of the bridge.

The man was standing in front of a tan Camry; the other, younger man by a large red SUV with a Princeton sticker on its back window.

"You mean someone's about to jump?"

"Yes."

"Can you see him?"

"Yes."

"Who is it?"

"One of us."

"Excuse me?"

"Us," said the man, gesturing with his right hand at the sea of cars, which extended back to the toll booths.

"It's a man?"

"Yes," said the man, putting down the binoculars, turning to size up the younger man, whose charcoal-gray, pinstripe Brooks Brothers suit went nicely with his orange and black tie, white shirt, and vest. The man himself was no longer young, yet he wore blue jeans, a black turtleneck, and a gray jacket.

"Young or old?"

"Younger than me, older than you."

"Those must be good binoculars."

"They are."

"Hey, this bridge is moving," said the younger man.

"Suspension," said the man, raising his binoculars, looking toward the city.

It was not a day to be out and about.

•••

"You're doin' fine, Jimmy; you're keepin' her nice and straight," said the father.

"I'm tryin', Dad," said the boy, who had a cushion underneath him so he could see over the windshield to steer his father's boat. The boy was 12, yet today he was doing a man's job.

"Jus' keep us in line, boy," said the other man seated opposite the father, both of them with lines out.

The 21-foot Barry Boat was one of five boats moving slowly across the bay at Cook's Dock on the northern part of the Manitoulin. A north wind of five knots drove a cold rain into the three in the boat.

Here, loggers brought trees from the bush, stripped off the bark on the beach, then dumped them into Lake Huron to be held by booms.

"Those booms, they came in handy, eh?" said the other man, who had a red face and a dirty neck.

The five boats were inside a grid made by the logging booms. They'd just started dragging.

"Yes, they did," said the father.

The father and the other man sat with their backs to the north wind.

"So you know this boy," said the other man, spitting tobacco juice nearly into the water. The juice dripped from the gunnel into the inside of the boat.

"Yes, yes, I did."

"Dad saved his life once," said Jimmy, looking over his shoulder at the two men behind him.

"That so?" said the other man, letting out more line.

The grappling hooks were down ten fathoms, bumping over rocks, tearing out the deep weeds where the pike lived.

"It was spring before last," said the father.

"We were tryin' out our new motor on Lake James," said Jimmy.

"Lake James? Where's that?"

"In Indiana, north of where we lived," said the boy. "So anyway, we just got started out on the lake and here comes this big boat with about a dozen old people in it, they were just out sightseein' or somethin' and they had a big wake behind them and…"

"Jimmy, larboard!" said the father.

"Sorry," said the boy, turning the boat.

"Keep a tack on that dock," said the father, pointing toward the cabin on the small island outside the bay.

"Go on," said the other man.

"So this tourist boat had this big wake and cuttin' across it came Robbie in a 12-foot Rinker with a 25-horse Merc…"

"Robbie, that's his name?" said the red-faced man.

"Robert McClure. Robbie," said the father.

"And so Robbie hit that wake goin' maybe 40 miles an hour and he was flipped out, but the Rinker had hit dead on, and it came back upright and kept on runnin…"

"How far away was you when he went over?"

"Close, like here to shore," said the boy, pointing toward Cook's Dock, about 25 yards away.

On the dock itself were two sets of parents, a truck that served as an ambulance when it wasn't used to haul logs, and seven or eight teenagers from Camp Normac.

"But you got to him in time," said the man.

"Just barely," the boy said. "I had to take over the steerin'. Robbie went under just as we got close..."

"He couldn't swim?"

"He had on hip boots, they filled up, pulled him down," said the father

"So I cut the motor, we drifted up to where he went under, and Dad got him by the hand."

"He fight ya?"

"No, he was dead tired," said the father.

"He said, 'Man, am I glad to see you, Teach'!" said the boy.

"So he was one of your students, eh?" said the other man.

"Yes, he was," said the father.

"You wouldn't think a boy like that, and him being a lifeguard, wouldn't be able to get to shore, especially when the girlie he had with him, she made it all right."

"Maybe he had on hip boots," said the boy.

"Maybe," said the father.

The five boats reached the end of a sweep. The grappling hooks were drawn in; they were cleaned of mud and weeds. The boats were now outside the point. The wind-driven cold rain stung the face of the boy as he steered the big, all-cedar Barry boat.

"We gonna make another pass? Don't seem like we're gettin' much of anywhere," said the other man.

"Nice and easy, Jimmy, get us in line," said the father as the boat tucked inside the point where the wind could no longer have at them.

The boy remembered the poem framed on the cedar wall of their main cabin:

"When the wind is from the north
The fisherman does not venture forth."

On such a day as this, with the wind and the spitting rain, only a pike would bite.

"Hair of the dog?" said the other man, offering a bottle to the father.

The boy turned and saw the man's dirty hand which gave way to a dirty wrist which in turn was half-covered by a dirty green wool shirt.

"Sure," said the father, taking a long pull from the bottle.

The boy turned back to the business of driving the boat. Behind him, he could hear the men drinking. He kept the big boat straight as an arrow.

•••

On the Verrazano, the rain was easing up.

"You think he'll jump?" said the younger man with the Princeton tie.

"I don't know," said the man.

"You ever seen this before?"

"Heard of it."

"Here?"

"Here, and on the George Washington, and on the Brooklyn Bridge."

"Any of them actually jump?"

"One did, from here, about 20 years ago."

"20 years! You've been commuting for that long?"

"Longer."

"This is only my second year, but I hate it."

"And you commute to?"

"Wall Street. You?"

"Brooklyn."

The traffic westbound on the bridge heading for New Jersey was stacked up with rubberneckers willing to extend their drive times to get a glimpse of human misery.

Most of the other eastbound drivers stayed in their cars.

"It'd be some job to get him out if he does jump," said the younger man.

"They'd have to dive."

"That'd be like finding a needle in a haystack. Where would they start?"

"Depends on how the current takes him, maybe over toward Coney Island, maybe into the harbor," said the man, focusing his binoculars on the lost soul hanging onto one of the bridge's many supports.

"The wind must be really blowing up there."

"Yes, it is," said the man.

•••

The rain cut into the boy's eyes. He blinked to see. They'd cleared the point again. They'd cleaned the grappling hooks again. The five boats were lined up for yet another pass.

"Engine caught on fire is how I heard it," said the other man, who put his line between his legs and rolled a cigarette. He spit out the tobacco he'd been chewing. Most of it cleared the boat.

"Best to keep both hands on the line," said the father.

"I'm OK," said the other man, sealing the cigarette by

licking across it with his tongue. He lit up, then let the handmade dangle from his lips.

"They had a seven-horse Martin Fisherman; its tank is hard to fill," said the boy.

"Shouldn't be out in a boat if you can't handle it," said the other man, resting his cigarette on a gunnel to free up a hand for another drink.

"He probably panicked. It could happen to any of us," said the father.

"All I know is, I can take care of myself out on the water," said the other man, drinking. Some of the whiskey ran down the stubble covering his chin.

"I'm sure you can," said the father, who took the bottle from the other man and drank.

"How long we gonna do this?" said Jimmy, watching his father drink.

"Until we find him," said the father.

"Holy Jesus! I got somethin'!" said the other man, dropping his cigarette into the lake, using both hands on the line.

"Cut the engine, Jimmy," said the father, tying his line to one of the seats.

The big Barry Boat came around as the other man's line tightened on what it had snagged.

"I got him! I got him!"

"Easy does it, you don't know where he's hooked," said the father.

The two men worked the line, the other man taking in hand over hand, the father coiling the line in the bottom of the boat.

The other four boats stopped sweeping, dropped

anchor, watched as the fifth boat brought in its catch.

The boy could see something coming to the surface. He'd seen big pike caught at Cook's Dock. He'd seen the pike hooked in the deep weeds and watched as they were fought to the surface.

Whatever was hooked on the other man's line did not fight as it was brought to the surface.

"There he is! God almighty! Look how swole up he is!" said the other man as the catch floated on the top of the cold water.

"Help me tie him to the side," said the father.

The other man could now see up close what he had caught. He could also smell what he had caught.

"Jimmy! Grab the feet! We're about to lose him!" said the father.

Jimmy stepped over the other man, who was on all fours in the bottom of the boat. The boy heard his heaving. The boy could smell and see what the other man had all over the front of his dirty green wool shirt; it ran down into the bottom of the boat.

"Oh God I'm gonna die!" moaned the other man.

"That's the way, Jimmy, use a slip knot," said the father as the boy secured the feet to the boat. The feet were inside hip boots which were cold and slick to the touch.

"Should I start the motor now?"

"Let me get my line in first, wouldn't want you to cut it," said the father, bringing in the rest of his line. His grappling hook was covered with mud and weeds. He put the line and the hook in the bottom of the boat.

"Get me to shore away from that thing!" said the other man, still on all fours on the shiny cedar floorboards of the boat. His words were hard to understand because of the dry heaves that came, and went, and came again.

"Start her up, Jimmy," said the father.

"To shore or to the dock?"

"The shore, beach it starboard, that way the water will keep him afloat."

Jimmy put the Barry Boat on the stone beach. The other man got out of the boat and headed, head down and with one hand on his stomach, toward the bush.

"We better not let them see him," said the father, looking toward the people from the dock as they made their way toward the boat.

"You go and stop them," said the boy.

"You be OK by yourself here?"

"I'll be OK."

Jimmy watched his father walk toward Robbie's parents.

Beside him, the corpse bobbed, face up, in the water. Jimmy stuck his hand in the water. It felt cold in the wet chill of the gray day. Jimmy looked at his slipknot. It would be easy to untie. He looked at the cedar floorboards of the boat. He'd have to clean out the boat. He looked at the face in the water. He could barely make out that it was Robbie's face.

The north wind shifted to the northeast and made its way deep into the bay at Cook's Dock. The wind rocked the boat.

Jimmy was sure he would've made it back to shore after the Martin Fisherman had caught fire.

•••

"There he goes," said the man.

The younger man joined other drivers who'd left their cars to rush to the edge of the bridge for a look-see at one of their own hitting the dead-cold, stone-hard water.

The man moved his binoculars toward New York harbor. Two boats were heading toward the bridge into a strong wind from the east.

As a boy, on an island, in another country, the man had read a poem framed on the varnished cedar walls of a cabin. One of its lines was:

"When the wind is from the east
The fishin' is the least."

The poem was about catching fish.

The man walked back to his car. He opened the door. He sat down. He put the binoculars into the glove compartment. He started the car. He took a cigar from a leather case. He lowered the left front window. He lit the cigar using a single wooden stove match. He did not let the flame touch the cigar. The man drew on the cigar.

He checked his watch. He was sure he would never do something like that. The cigar tasted foul in his mouth. The man threw the cigar out the window. He checked his watch again. The traffic jam would soon open up.

The Ledge

The fire from the canoe took the nip from the air.

"So glad you could come, Jimmy," said the woman, looking up at the man, smiling. Her eyes reflected the fire that had just started behind the man.

"Glad I could make it," said the man, who could feel on his neck the heat from the fire.

In all, twelve people, an even dozen, stood in a half-circle, facing Silver Lake at twilight. It was late August on the Manitoulin, cool, already in the 50s.

"Jimmy, this is my husband, Charles Chauncey," said the woman, whose short, blond hair framed her tanned face.

"So, you're Jim," said the tall, mostly Eddie-Bauered man by her side, offering his hand. He too had short, blond hair and a George Hamilton tan.

"Yes, I am. And that's your daughter," said the man, shaking the husband's hand, feeling its strength. He released the husband's hand and looked past the two blondes at the blonde teenager standing outside the half-circle.

"Oh yes, that's my Carol," said the woman.

The man smiled. Carol, not Carolyn like the mother.

"This was the way your father wanted it to be," said the husband to his wife as they and the other nine looked at the canoe now burning at both ends.

"It's just exactly what I promised Daddy," said the woman, holding her husband's hand tightly.

The man did not turn around.

He had known the canoe during its lifetime.

•••

"You've handled a canoe before, haven't you, Jimmy?" said Carolyn Long's father, peering at the boy over his bifocals.

"Oh sure, lots of times," said Jimmy.

"Wouldn't want to have to come to the rescue of you two kids," said the father.

"No problem, we'll be OK."

"Don't worry, Daddy, Jimmy will take care of me," said Carolyn Long, who kissed her father good-bye, then walked toward the canoe beached on the shore.

Jimmy followed the girl. She had on short white shorts and a large floppy red Indiana University T-shirt. Her deep tan made the short white shorts even whiter.

"So, this is your canoe," said Jimmy, who had never been in a canoe in his life.

"This is it. Daddy built it himself."

The boy had seen, yesterday, a picture of a canoe in the Peterborough Canoe catalogue. A man with big arms was at one end while a woman with blown-back black hair sat toward the front with a small brown and white dog and helped paddle. In the picture, canoeing looked easy.

"He built it himself?"

"Yes, it's got some wooden frame thingy and every year Daddy paints the canvas and varnishes the inside. Doesn't it smell great?"

"Yeah, great," said the boy, recalling that in the catalogue there was a canoe, reasonably priced, called the Floatwell, about 16 feet long, a yard at the beam, with something called sponsons in it so its passengers stayed on the upside of a lake.

"This thing have sponsons in it?"

"What?"

"Never mind," said the boy, feeling the approach of Mr. Long.

The boy and the girl pushed the canoe into the lake, she in first, the boy turning it into the wind, guiding it from the rear, then using his legs to one-step inside.

"Wave to Daddy," said Carolyn Long, turning around, making the canoe rock to one side.

Jimmy gave three waves of his left hand; the right he kept on the paddle. He did not turn around.

•••

"You came all the way from New York to see this?" said Carolyn Long's daughter, her face lit by the fire coming from the canoe.

The man looked at the girl. Same blond hair, same tan, same short white shorts, the same red Indiana University T-shirt.

"Yes."

"Why?"

"I knew your grandfather when I was a boy."

"You know, it's kind of creepy to do this."

"It was in his will."

"Still and all, it's creepy; first they throw his ashes in the lake, then they burn his canoe."

"You go to IU?"

"Not yet, I'm only a junior."

The man did the math.

"Sixteen is a good age to be."

"You think so?"

"Sure."

"You used to come up here, didn't you?" said Carol Long.

"Yes."

"That's your old place over there, isn't it?" said the daughter, pointing through the birch trees close to shore at the three white cabins in the center of the bay.

"Yes," said the man, who could've turned and seen the cabins in the moonlight.

•••

"You can really handle a canoe, Jimmy," said Carolyn Long.

"Thanks," said Jimmy, happy she had her back to him and couldn't see the times he'd twisted the paddle, making it enter the water at the wrong angle.

"Where we going?"

"The Ledge."

"Anywhere else?"

"After we fish for a while, we can picnic at Turnbull's Point. I brought food, and a blanket."

"Great." Carolyn Long turned to smile at him, her teeth white against the brown of her tan, the wind blowing back her short blond hair.

•••

The fire was making its way from each end of the canoe, lusting after its other half.

"You know Mom from way back, don't you?" said Carol Long.

"Yes."

"What was it like up here then?"

"Less crowded. No electricity, no phones, grass in the middle of the road."

"So I guess you two hung out together?"

"Sometimes."

•••

The canoe had made it, upright, to the middle of the lake.

"We're here," said Jimmy.

"How can you tell?" said Carolyn Long.

"You line up the white corner post on Merrick's house with a scrub pine on the shore, then you track in line toward the highest maple on Turnbull's Point."

"You know a lot of stuff, Jimmy."

"I try," said the boy, using a sinker on his fishing line to find the dead center of the Ledge.

"I can see it!" said the girl, leaning over the canoe on the same side as the boy.

"Careful, this thing's tippy."

"I don't have to worry, you'd save me if we capsized," said the girl, smiling at the boy with the tip of her tongue peeking out. The boy snagged the line as he stared at her.

"Yeah, I'd save you," said Jimmy, looking from her to his canvas bag in which he had their lunch and his preparations. He'd brought one pillow, one blanket, one book of poems, one bottle of Peppermint Schnapps taken from his father's liquor cabinet, and two condoms.

"Oh, it's hot," said Carolyn Long, taking off her T-shirt. The black of her two-piece contrasted nicely with her tan.

"Yeah, really hot," said Jimmy, looking at her as he let the anchor down to the right of the Ledge, which had been formed by the Wisconsin Glacier and amounted to a rock rising from the bottom to within five feet of the surface. The Ledge was a good place to fish. Six feet wide, 15 feet long, it was hard to find, but the boy had followed his father's instructions to the letter.

"Cigarette?"

"I'd love one."

Carolyn Long held his hand while he lit her cigarette; a moment later she blew her smoke gently in his face.

"Hope the fish are biting," said the boy.

"Me, too," said the girl.

•••

"Oh, look at that!" said Carol Long as the flames met

in the middle of the canoe.

"It's the varnish," said the man.

"It's cold, even with the fire," she said, moving closer to the man.

He took off his jacket and placed it over her shoulders.

The man lit a cigarette.

"No one we know smokes."

"Hard to smoke when you're eating tofu," said the man.

"That's funny," she said, laughing, watching the man smoke.

"Did Mom smoke?"

"Yes."

"With you?"

"Yes," said the man, looking over the daughter's shoulder at Carolyn Long and her husband and their friends, all of them come to this place to honor the past.

•••

"I've got another one!" said the girl.

"Bring him this way," said Jimmy, who grabbed the line and pulled the smallmouth into the canoe.

"We've done all right," said Carolyn.

"Yes, we have." Jimmy wished the fish would stop biting so they could get on with the rest of the afternoon. All summer he'd planned for this day; he'd even written a poem:

"To have a girl of your charms
To hold in my arms
Is…"

The last line he was still working on.

"How many do we have?"

"Four, all of them keepers," said Jimmy.

"Let me see," said the girl, leaning far over the side of the canoe where the boy had hung the stringer.

The boy weighed 200 pounds, the girl 110, which meant that Mr. Long's handmade homemade canoe at that moment had 310 pounds on its right gunnel. And no sponsons.

The canoe capsized.

•••

"It'll soon be nothing but ashes," said the daughter of Carolyn Long.

"Yes."

"Can I have one tiny drag?"

"Your mother approve?"

"She's watchin' the fire."

Carol Long put her left hand on the man's right while she drew on his cigarette, then blew smoke gently into his face.

•••

The cold of the water shocked the boy. Back at the surface, he looked for the girl.

"Jimmy! Jimmy!" She was close by, maybe 20 feet from the Ledge. Swimming toward her, the boy could see the canvas canoe, drifting south, back toward the Longs' cabin, which was three miles downwind.

"I've got you, you're safe," said the boy, wrapping his

right hand around her, then under her right arm, grabbing her left shoulder, pulling her body onto his.

The girl didn't fight him. He took one scissors kick; he moved the two of them toward the Ledge.

"Jimmy! What'll we do, I can't swim all the way home!" gasped Carolyn Long.

"It's all right," said Jimmy, using his left arm to get up some speed. He had his right leg under her; he used his left to feel for the bottom. His toes brushed something, then his foot was hitting rock.

The boy put his weight onto first his left leg, then his right. He stood. He was in the middle of the Ledge. The boy was just about six-foot-three; he put both arms under Carolyn Long to keep her head above water.

"The canoe's way far away," said the girl.

"I know."

At the three cabins owned by the boy's parents, Jimmy's father was asleep in the storage cabin. A plump, golden puppy named Wicky slept at the father's feet.

An older dog, Mike, sat at the cabin door, ears up, looking at the lake.

At the girl's cabin, Mr. Long checked his watch. They'd been gone just two hours.

The canoe drifted slowly toward the shore. The wind blew gently. It would be some time before the fathers found the canoe.

In the middle of Silver Lake, in July, on the Ledge, Jimmy held Carolyn Long in his arms.

•••

The canoe was now, in the main, embers.

"It's over," said the daughter, taking one long, last draw on the man's cigarette.

"He was a good man, I liked him," said the man.

"But you came here to see Mom, didn't you?" said Carol Long.

"Yes."

"You're the one she told me about."

The man lit a new cigarette.

"When we had our heart-to-heart talk about, you know, she said there was someone before Daddy."

The canoe was now all ashes. Carolyn Long and her husband and their friends scooped the ashes into tin buckets.

"That was a long time ago."

"But the two of you, you remember one another."

"Yes."

"Cool."

"Shall we go and gather ashes?"

"You ever go back there?" said the daughter, pointing again toward the three white cabins.

The man turned and looked at the cabins.

"No one can go back there."

"Why not?"

"That's the past. A bad place the past. The best place is..."

"The future?"

"No, the present. There's nothing better than the present."

"You have a son?"

"Yes."

"My age?"

"Close enough."

"Can I meet him?

"Why not?"

"That'd be cool, wouldn't it?"

"I guess," said the man as he walked with Carolyn Long's daughter to collect the ashes of the past.

Husbands

"Isn't he cute?" said the wife. She was short and thin, her hair blacker than nature had intended.

"To whom?" said the tall man wearing Armani sunglasses, whose thinning-on-top black hair was brushed back from a deeply tanned forehead.

"What?"

"It's an animal," said the man.

"Yeah, that's what I told her," said the wife's husband, looking up at the man.

The three were three yards from the bear pit, but one of the bear cubs could clearly be seen since it had climbed a scrub pine at the edge of the pit.

"You been up this way before?" said the wife's husband.

"Yes," said the man, looking down at the short, fat husband, who'd spent some time in the morning combing his hair to hide his bald spot.

"We're on our way to someplace called Sudbury. Where's that road go?" said the husband, pointing toward a sign that read Route 6.

"Espanola."

"What kinda place is that?" said the wife.

Queens or Long Island, thought the man. He'd bet a week's pay on his being right.

"An old logging town. Now it's mostly for tourists on the way to the Manitoulin."

"Where?" said the wife.

"Manitoulin. Manitoulin Island; it's where the road goes."

"Sounds like an Indian name, like something we got back home," said the husband.

"Mineola?" said the man.

"How'd you know where we were from?" said the husband.

"Lucky guess," said the man, depositing the bet he'd made with himself.

"So, what's on this island?" said the wife.

"Cows, snakes, bears."

"You're joking."

"Also tourists."

"Like us?" said the husband.

"Yes," said the man, looking past the couple from Long Island at those who'd stopped at the intersection of 17 and 6 on their way to or from the Sault or Sudbury.

The bear pit wasn't the only attraction. The enterprising owner sold Christmas ornaments, even at this time in June, plus products, genuine, made by the "First Peoples of Canada."

The man had stopped for gas. Old habits die hard. Long ago, this had been the last gas stop open at all hours. Even in Espanola the stations had closed early.

•••

"Got to gas up, Jimmy, wouldn't want to run out near the nuthouse," the boy's father had said.

"There really a nuthouse in those hills?" said Jimmy.

"Yes, there is. Right in the middle of 40 miles of bad road. I want us full to the gills," said the father.

"Anything else in the hills?" said Jimmy.

"Bears,"said the father.

•••

"This should keep them happy," said the father, working on a Browning Auto-Five he held across his lap.

"Nothin' much else for them to do," said Jimmy, steering the boat, his left hand on the throttle of a ten-horsepower Mercury Hurricane, the other on the right gunnel.

The father sat in the middle of the 16-foot Peterborough Fisherman; behind him, at the bow, were two Golden Retrievers, one four years old, the other one, each of them with a snout over a gunnel, snapping at waves.

"What they thought they were doin' coming up here at this time of year is beyond me."

"But they still have to pay to stay with us, don't they?"

"Yes, they do," said the father.

"Good," said Jimmy, looking over his shoulder at the other, smaller, Peterborough riding in their wake, with a lanky wife in the middle and a heavyset husband at the helm.

"Skeet or trap?" said Jimmy, watching as his father

adjusted the choke.

"Skeet," said the father.

"Safer?"

"Yes, anyone can shoot up."

"Even a husband?"

"Even a husband," said the father, laughing.

The boy liked to hear his father laugh. It felt good to be out on the water. A west wind was making small whitecaps; the sky was a bright blue; there were no clouds. It was a good day to fish. In the main cabin they'd just left there was a poem framed on a cedar wall:

"When the wind is from the west
The fishin' is the best."

Words of wisdom. Only, in June on the Manitoulin, no one could fish for smallmouth bass. Tourists soon got bored with catching perch and pitching horseshoes. On the north side of Silver Lake, the husband and wife could shoot. There were no roads to the north side; no game warden could come at the sound of a shot to see if someone had taken a deer out of season.

"She be able to handle the .22?" said Jimmy, staring at the bolt-action Remington beside his father, who also carried a Colt .45 in a holster.

"That'll be your job."

"And you get the husband?"

"I get the husband."

"Lucky you."

"Yes, lucky me," said the father, laughing again.

•••

"Oh, look, he's fallen," said the Long Island wife, laughing at the cub, who'd tumbled out of the pine.

"His mother don't seem too happy," said the husband.

"No, she doesn't," said the man, looking at the she-bear, who was looking at the tourist laughing at her cub.

The man had seen that look before.

•••

"Good shot," said Jimmy, as the wife hit the target dead center.

"You're a good teacher," said the wife, using the bolt action to rack in another bullet. Her nails were clipped short and unpainted.

Jimmy looked toward the two cedar boats beached on the sandy shore.

To the right of the boats near the swamp, the two Goldens, Mike and Wicky, were catching minnows. Mike slapped at the water with his paws while Wicky snapped at the dead minnows killed by Mike. Then both dogs stopped fishing.

"Here, Mike; here, Wicky," said Jimmy, speaking the commands clearly and concisely.

"Why do you want them over here?" said the wife.

"Put your rifle down," said Jimmy.

"Why?"

"Dad!" said Jimmy.

"What!" said the father, who was 50 yards away launching skeet for the husband, who had, to this point, hit one of ten.

"Bears!" said Jimmy.

The father looked at the lake.

A small bear cub was headed their way, pursued by Wicky. Mike wasn't chasing the cub. Mike was watching the two other bears. One of them was the mother. She was chasing Wicky, and trailing behind her was another cub. The five animals formed a parade. The cub first, then Wicky, the she-bear after him, Mike off to one side, and the other cub hightailing it after its mommy.

"Give me your rifle," said Jimmy.

The wife gave the boy the bolt-action Remington. The boy looked at the rifle. Useless. A .22 would only anger the she-bear.

The second cub was 15 yards from the husband when he fired three shots in five seconds. The cub yelped, rolled over and over, tried to stand on one of its bleeding front legs, fell. The cub kept trying to get up.

The she-bear turned, headed for her cub.

"Mike, come here!" said the father.

Mike came.

"Get Wicky," the father said to Jimmy as he took the Browning Auto-Five from the husband.

"Get in your boat," he told the husband and the wife.

The husband held his wife's hand as they ran toward the Peterborough on the shore.

Jimmy looked at Wicky losing ground on the cub, which was running a circle which would take him, and the Golden, back to the she-bear. There were five yards between the cub and the dog. Jimmy fired into that space, kicking up dust.

"Wicky! Wicky!"

The dog stopped chasing the cub.

"Wicky, come here!"

The dog came to the boy.

The father had Mike, the boy had Wicky, and the husband and the wife were on the lake headed back toward the cabin.

The hot June sun beat down.

The father and the son watched the she-bear and her cubs.

•••

"Ever see one of those things on the outside?" said the husband from Mineola.

"Yes," said the man.

"I wouldn't like to meet up with her," said the husband, looking down at the she-bear, who had gathered in her cub but still stared at the tourists.

"Neither did I," said the man.

•••

"What'll we do?" said Jimmy.

"That cub is going to die," said the father.

"But not for a while."

"No, not for a while."

The cub was down. They could hear it whimpering. The mother licked at its wounds.

The other cub was three yards from its brother and its mother.

"Anyone comin' this way?" said the father.

"No," said Jimmy, scanning the lake for the game warden.

The remaining Peterborough was still beached. They had a clear path to the boat.

The boy held the Remington; the father had the Browning and the .45.

"Can you put one between her and the other cub?"

"Nick him?"

"No. Make him run."

Jimmy levered a shell into the chamber.

"Wicky, stay," he said, then shot over the sitting dog.

Dust kicked up next to the cub. It started to run, away from the mother and the injured cub, toward the bush.

The mother looked their way. If looks could kill, they would have been dead. She ran after the second cub.

"Good boy," said the father, walking to the boat.

"Wicky, heel," said Jimmy, grabbing the younger dog by its choke collar, making it walk by his side.

Mike walked, without being told, in heel mode by the father's side.

"Mike, in," said the father.

The older Golden jumped into the boat. The boy helped Wicky in.

The boy put the Remington .22 into the boat.

"You take this," said the father, handing the boy the Browning. The father still had the .45 in its holster.

The boy knew the legend of the .45. It, supposedly, could put a 200-pound man on the ground even if he were hit on the tip of the finger. There was nothing in the legend about what a she-bear would do when hit.

"She'll come back once she catches him," said Jimmy.

"I know," said the father, taking a five-gallon gas can from the Peterborough.

The father and his son walked to where the cub lay. It was still alive, but barely. The grass all around it was wet and red.

"If she comes, you put down a field of fire in front of her. Not all at once. Make her stop. All you're doing is buyin' time," said the father as he removed the .45 from his holster.

"Let me kill it," said Jimmy.

"Why?"

"I'm a kid. If we get caught they'll do nothin' to me."

"You OK to do this?"

"I'm OK."

The father and the son switched guns. The father took the Browning Auto-Five, the boy the .45.

The pistol felt cold in the boy's hand. The sun felt hot on his neck. He looked down at the cub; its eyes were open, looking up at him; its pink tongue was far out of its mouth. The boy could hear its ragged breathing.

The husband had missed with shot number one, but shot number two had brought the bear cub down with a hit to the front leg. The real damage had been done by shot number three, though. The cub was gutshot. It would take it some time to die.

Jimmy shot the cub between the eyes. Something hot hit his forehead.

"Stand back," said the father, who doused the cub with gasoline.

"She's comin' back!" said Jimmy, hearing a noise from the bush.

The father dropped a match onto a paper he'd placed next to the cub. Flames made their way from the paper to the gasoline.

The boy and his father ran for the boat. Jimmy could hear the mother coming through the bush.

"Push us out," said the father at the helm, priming the Mercury.

Jimmy pushed the boat from the beach.

"Get in," said the father.

The father started the Mercury Hurricane with one pull.

Jimmy looked at the north shore. There was a blaze in the meadow. There was a cub at the edge of the bush. And there was a she-bear circling the fire.

"We're away," said Jimmy.

"Yes, we are," said the father, staring at his son.

"What's the matter?" said Jimmy, looking at his father.

"Wash your forehead."

Jimmy dipped his hand in the water, brought it to his face. The water was cold. Red ran down his hand.

"Again," said the father.

Jimmy rubbed his face until no more red ran down his hand.

"Think they'll say anything?"

"What's for them to say? They'd have to confess. Why would they do that?"

"Game warden get onto us?"

"You never know. We'll lie low. Mum will be the word. Maybe all of this will pass," said the father.

He turned up the throttle on the Mercury Hurricane. With the two Goldens toward the bow, the Peterborough started to plane. A half mile ahead, the boy could see the second boat carrying the husband and the wife to the safety of the south shore.

Jimmy watched the scene on the north shore become smaller and smaller.

•••

The wife from Mineola walked away from the bear pit toward the gift shop.

"Grr," said a fat boy of maybe nine, who was holding his mother's hand.

"Grr."

The she-bear looked at the boy.

"She'd like to get ahold of him," said the husband quietly.

"Yes, she would," said the man, looking at the cub huddled next to its mother.

"So there's nothin' to see on the way to, what'd you call it, Espanola?"

"Not much."

"And not a lot to see on that island?"

"You and your wife like to fish?"

"No."

"Flora and fauna of any interest to you two?"

"Not really."

"Horseshoes?"

"Never actually done that."

"Sudbury has some outlet stores."

"That'd be great for my wife."

"Grr," said the fat boy.

"She can't get at him, but she can't get hurt, either," said the husband, staring at the she-bear.

"No, she can't."

"I guess where she is is about the right place for bears these days."

"Yes, it is."

"Nice to have met you," said the husband, extending his hand.

The man shook the husband's hand.

"You going to the island?"

"Yes," said the man.

"Gonna visit friends and relatives?"

"No," said the man.

"You lookin' for somethin' special?"

"Yes," said the man.

"What?"

"Yesterday," said the man, leaving the husband and walking toward his car. He checked his watch. He'd be on the island before dark. The 40 miles of bad road through the LeCloche Mountains had been blasted into a straight highway. He didn't know if the nuthouse was still there.

He didn't think bears lived there anymore, either.

Wives

"Best not to do that," said the man.

"Why not?" said the short fat freckled girl, flicking her hand at the yellow and black wasp.

"There're more where he came from."

The man watched the yellowjacket forage for food. In June, the search would've been for flies; now the wasp was after sugars. It crawled over the raspberry and rhubarb pie on the picnic table.

"Get away from it!" said the girl's mother, who was a big-below-the-waist woman.

The mother held a large plastic spoon in a meaty hand. With it she crushed the yellowjacket.

The man sat alone at an adjacent picnic table. From a leather case, he took out a cigar. He used a wooden stove match to toast the end of the cigar. He rolled the cigar as he lit it. He did not let the flame touch the cigar.

It would not take long.

The man knew a thing or two about yellowjackets.

•••

"And the bathroom is where?" said the wife, who was not old but who, in aging, had grown large in visible places.

"It's down that path," said Jimmy, pointing toward the bush.

"You're kidding," said the wife.

"No, he's not kidding," said Jimmy's father.

Jimmy hoped his father would not tell his privy jokes.

One of them involved a carpenter well known for his outhouses.

It was not a long story, but it took the father some time to tell it.

'Guaranteed odor-free or your money back' was the carpenter's motto. And, once upon a time in a faraway land, the carpenter had built a fresh-cut, all-cedar outhouse for a woman new to the area. Within two weeks she was back to the carpenter.

'It stinks,' she said.

'Impossible, madam, this has never happened before.'

The woman demanded the carpenter inspect the outhouse. Which he did.

'Well?' the woman had said.

'Madam, of course it stinks,' the carpenter replied, 'for you have SHAT in it.'

The other joke was actually a poem. The poem wasn't very long, but it usually took the father quite a while to recite it.

The poem's title was: "When Lightning Struck the Outhouse."

The poem's best line was:

'The wind she blew,
And the shit, it flew.'

"No one on this end of the island has indoor plumbing," said the father.

"It'll be ok, Gracie, it'll be like camping out," said the wife's husband, who was short and thin and looked like he said "yes" a lot.

"It'll have to do," said the wife, turning and walking toward the guest cabin. She wore sky-blue Bermuda shorts that strained at the seams.

•••

The man smoked his cigar. It was his second cigar of the day. He had bought several cigars the day before in Toronto. Canada had no problem with Castro. Good for them, thought the man.

"You like to smoke?" said the girl, who had been left at the picnic table. Her mother and a brother of maybe six or seven had walked to the shore, which was not far from the small park with picnic tables secured by the Reeve for Gore Bay. The mother wore a green-with-large-yellow-flowers one-piece bathing suit.

"Yes."

"Why?"

"Protection," said the man.

"From what?"

"Them," said the man, pointing to the swarms at the shore. Yellowjackets are social insects. Someone had disturbed their nest.

"My mother could get stung," said the girl.

"Yes, she could," said the man.

•••

"Jimmy! There's trouble outside," said the boy's mother, sitting at a table, her walker by her side, shucking peas.

"What kind of trouble?" said Jimmy. He was in the kitchen, using the hand pump to fill a bucket with water.

"You won't know until you go look."

"Where's Dad?"

"You'll have to take care of this yourself," said the mother.

Jimmy emptied the bucket into the reservoir of the cast-iron Master Climax wood stove.

Once outside, he had no trouble finding the trouble. He went to where the screaming was the loudest.

"Help me! Oh God! Maurice! Maurice! Help me!" yelled the wife, who was running in circles in the open field beyond the outhouse. Her sky-blue Bermudas were at half-mast. The hot summer sun shone on her ample white buttocks.

Several yellowjackets pursued the wife.

"What'll we do!" said the husband, staring, wide-eyed, at the boy.

"Get her to come this way," said Jimmy.

"How?"

"Use this to cover her up from the wasps," said Jimmy, handing the husband a large white beach towel he'd taken from the clothesline.

The husband, beach towel in hand, ran into the field after the wife.

The boy went to the porch of the guest cabin. He removed ice from the icebox. He placed the ice in a bucket. He looked toward the field at the running wife. He would need a bigger bucket.

"I got her! I got her!" said the husband, running behind his wife, hands on her shoulders, urging the big woman onward. Her head was covered with the white beach towel. The yellowjackets honed in on where the towel wasn't.

Jimmy removed a raspberry and rhubarb pie from the icebox. He dumped it onto the ground.

"Bring her this way," said Jimmy, walking toward the horseshoe pit.

The husband brought the wife. Jimmy pulled out a horseshoe stake. Into a sandy pit he dumped the ice.

"Down," he said.

"Down?" said the husband.

"Oh God does it sting!" said the wife.

"Down," said the boy.

The wife squatted, lowering her broad bare behind into the ice in the horsehoe pit.

The wasps could no longer smell the odor of their own stings. They could smell the raspberry and rhubarb pie. They went for the pie.

•••

"Oh my God! Help me!" screamed the mother as she kicked her leg.

Lou "the toe" Groza had never kicked higher. Off went her shoe.

"Mother got stung!" said the girl.

"Yes, she did," said the man, watching as the mother ran in circles. Her son was already in the water.

"What'll we do?"

"Get help," said the man, moving over to the other table, taking the raspberry and rhubarb pie and throwing it away from him, toward the shore.

"Where?"

"There," said the man, pointing toward the main street of Gore Bay.

The girl ran for help.

The man had not seen the street for some time. In his day there'd been mostly a hardware store called Boyd's which largely sold fishing gear, an Esso station, a butcher shop run by a big guy named Barney, the Marvel Tea Room, Smith's where his mother had bought a Hudson Bay blanket for him, Marv Wood's restaurant (hamburgs a specialty), the Bank of Montreal, the Co-Op where they got feed for their chickens, and a grocery called the Central Store. The OPP (Ontario Provincial Police department) had been at the end of the street. He hoped it was still there.

The man watched the mother run. The yellowjackets were in hot pursuit. They'd found the one who'd done in Louie, who'd been sent on pie detail.

"Help me! Help me! Someone help me!"

"Head for the water," called the man.

The mother headed for the water.

"Dive," said the man.

The mother dove.

The man drew on his Lusitania. There was still a lot to be smoked.

He drank his coffee. It was coffee made from clear, clean Canadian water. He'd laced it with heavy cream and Jameson's. It went well with the cigar.

The mother and the son were under the water. The yellowjackets circled. They could no longer smell the odor of their stings. They could smell the raspberry and rhubarb pie. They made a beeline for the pie.

•••

"You ok, Gracie?" said the husband.

"It still stings," said the wife.

Jimmy looked at the wife in the horseshoe pit. He had once seen, in a magazine, a sumo wrestler. Before a match, the sumo wrestlers squatted before one another, then charged.

Jimmy took a step backward from the pit.

"How will you kill those things?" asked the husband.

"Wait until dark."

"What if you can't find them?"

"Wait until winter."

"What kinda place you running here!!" shrieked the wife.

"Cheap," said Jimmy.

The yellowjackets worked on the raspberry and rhubarb pie.

The boy was done here. He'd taken care of this himself. He'd not been forced to go to the storage cabin to get his father. The sun beat down. It was hot. The wind was from the south.

In the main cabin, on a cedar wall, was framed a poem:

"When the wind is from the south
The bait blows in the fish's mouth."
"Want more ice, Gracie?" said the husband.
"Yes," said the wife.
The boy left them to go fishing.

•••

"How will they kill them?" said the girl.

"Sevin," said the man, watching the first aid squad work on the woman.

The yellowjackets had been very angry. Yellowjackets don't die after one sting. The mother screamed while ice was applied to her leg. The little boy had not been stung.

"What's Sevin?"

"Poison."

"The bees were in the ground?"

"They're not bees. They're yellowjackets."

"What's the difference?"

"They make their nests in ratholes."

"Gross."

"Do you like it up here?"

"No, I hate it, this place sucks. Mother made us come."

"Where are you from?"

"Hamilton Square."

"In New Jersey."

"How'd you know that?"

"Lucky guess," said the man, who'd lived in New Jersey for 30 years.

"We wanted to go to Six Flags."

"Maybe next year," said the man, standing up.

He'd finished the coffee. The Lusitania was smoked nearly to the red-and-gold band.

He walked away from the park. The wind was from the south. He checked his watch: 4 p.m.

Maybe he would go fishing.

Torchlight

"Is it worth all this wait?" said a short, very tanned, very J. Crew woman.

"Yes," said the man.

"We're here because our husbands deserted us," said the woman's friend, giggling. She was taller, but still not tall, a brunette not a blonde; both women were in their mid-30s, trailing clouds of upward mobility.

"Really," said the man.

"No, no, she's just kidding. They've gone fishing; we came here because we heard about the maple syrup," said the blonde.

"What did you hear?"

"That it's better than what you can buy in Vermont; at least that's what we were told."

"Who told you?"

"Our hosts. We're staying at Sykes' on Silver Lake. Are you visiting up here?"

The man made the update. In his day, Sykes Lodge

had been the Ridley Lodge, which was where those from the States with less than deep pockets came to stay on Manitoulin Island for a Canadian vacation. Back then, in the 50s, the West End of the Manitoulin was for the rich; the East End for the rest. Looking at the two women, he determined that either East and West had met or the husbands were cheapskates.

"Yes," said the man.

"From where?"

"Brooklyn."

"Oh!" said the brunette.

"We never met anyone from Brooklyn before," said the blonde.

"And you're from?"

"Fort Wayne. It's in Indiana, you probably never heard of it."

The man, born and raised on the north side of Fort Wayne, had parked next to a SUV with Indiana plates beginning with the number two, which he recognized as from his hometown.

"Lots of cornfields, herds of buffalo roaming about?" said the man.

Both women laughed, the brunette loud enough to turn the heads of some of the other tourists who'd come to Meldrum Bay on a hot June afternoon to buy maple syrup at the Pickett farm.

"See that old man sitting at the back? Isn't he something?" said the blonde.

The man was now far enough inside the barn so he could see the figure, quietly rocking in his chair while someone who was probably his granddaughter dispensed maple syrup in gallon tins to fat-avoidant tourists, who'd need a decade to metabolize it.

"He hasn't changed," said the man, more to himself than to the two women.

"You know him?" said the blonde, looking up at the man, waiting for him to reply.

The old man in the rocking chair wore logging boots, navy blue Big Yank overalls, and—even though it was the last week of June—white long-johns. A red cotton long-sleeve shirt was buttoned at the collar and at both wrists. A wine-red cap pulled low on the ears contrasted with silver gray hair. Red scar tissue covered both cheeks all the way up to the high cheekbones. The middle of the face was without the scars, but it was weathered. It was a face that had spent most of its time outside. He stared at the line of tourists, eyes unblinking, his big, red scarred hands at rest on the arms of the rocker.

The man knew all about those hands.

"I knew him long ago," said the man.

•••

"Jimmy will take you to your cabin," said the father.

The guests—one tall thin husband; one tall thin wife; one short fat girl with pimples, age 11—stood to leave.

Jimmy's mother did not stand up.

"Use these to light the lamp," said the father, handing the boy a box of stove matches.

The boy took the matches quickly. He was sure the guests hadn't noticed the shaking of his father's hands.

"A lovely meal," said the wife to the mother, who used

her walker to rise slowly.

"Thank you," said the mother, on her feet, using the walker for balance. The boy hoped the guests thought the walker was because she'd had an injury. The answer, however, lay elsewhere.

•••

The boy shone his Captain Midnight pistol/flashlight on the book so he could read it. It was not easy reading.

"Jimmy! What're you doin' down here?" said his mother.

"Reading."

"Reading! At this hour! About what?"

"About what you got."

The mother was sitting up in bed. She'd turned on a light. She still had on the clothes she'd worn to the doctor's.

"That book answer your questions?"

"No."

"What do you want to know?"

"Is it catching?"

The mother said nothing. It was cold in the room. Moonlight shone through the lace curtains.

"Come here, Jimmy, sit by me."

The boy sat by his mother. They were in a dining room which had no dining room table, no dining chairs, and no sideboard. The boy and his mother sat on a small bed; next to the bed were a night table and a walker.

"No, what I have isn't catching."

"How did you get it?"

"It's inherited. If parents have it, then their children

can get it."

"So I could get sick, too?"

The mother went silent again. When she spoke, the words came out slowly, like she didn't want to release them.

"Jimmy, did you ever wonder why you don't look like your father?"

"You mean because I'm not fat?"

"No, no, I mean his face, the color of his eyes, his red hair. That sort of thing."

"I don't get you."

The mother took a deep breath, let it out slowly. Now the words came out rapid fire.

"You know, Jimmy…well, probably you don't know… that Johnny and Janet next door aren't the natural children of Mr. and Mrs. Evans…"

"They're not?"

"Listen to me. Don't interrupt. Johnny and Janet are, are adopted and… so are you."

"That means I was picked out from someplace."

"That's right."

"You mean like Daddy picked out Mike."

"Yes, that's one way of putting it. You're special. Just like Mike."

"So this means I can't catch what you have and I can't inherit it."

"That's right."

"So I'm OK."

"You're OK," said the mother, who turned off the light. She lay down slowly on the bed, drew up her legs, rolled away from her son.

The boy made his way upstairs. He took care to be

quiet. His father slept light. Any slight noise and he'd be up, and he'd stay up for most of the night. The father would not be happy if the boy woke him up.

In bed, the boy tried to put two and two together. Most of what he had read about Multiple Sclerosis didn't sound good, and the adoption business had been news to him. But his mother had straightened him out. Mike was a Champion. Mike had been voted best Golden Retriever for 1958. The boy became sleepy. He was OK. He was like Mike. The boy fell asleep.

•••

The boy held the door for the three guests. A big Golden Retriever was waiting outside.

"It's ok, Mike, they're with me," said the boy.

Behind him, the boy heard his father whisper "husbands," their code word for the male guests who came to the Manitoulin knowing little about life in the outdoors and acting with confidence on their ignorance.

Last summer, the father and the son had taken a husband fishing on the big lake. At Walkhouse Bay, the husband had caught a ten-pound Northern, not a trophy but a keeper, nonetheless. In the boat, the boy calmed the pike with a tap behind its neck from an axe-handle. He used his spreaders to open the mouth and reached for his needle-nose pliers but was too late; the husband had reached in to free the red-and-white daredevil lure. Drawing out his hand past the razor-sharp pike teeth, the husband, for an instant, still had a hand, then it was mostly blood. During the return to shore, the fingers became sausages; by the time they'd driven the 40 miles to the hospital at Mindemoya, the hand was a balloon.

The husband had made a lot of noise for most of the trip.

Outside, Mike led the way, followed by the boy, who walked fast. It was the last week of June but the black flies were still out and about. A half-ton truck, nearly rusted through below its doors, pulled into the driveway. The boy flashed his light toward the truck.

"Who's that?" said the wife.

"Mr. Pickett. He sells maple syrup. Once I get your light on, maybe he'll come to see you. Would that be OK?"

"Why not?' said the husband.

Mike, Jimmy, and the guests continued toward the sleeping cabin.

Inside the main cabin, the mother made her way slowly toward her bedroom. The father had already gone to the storage cabin, taking with him the younger dog named Wicky.

•••

"So, you've been up here before. My name's Sharon, this is my friend Marla," said the blonde.

"Jim," said the man, shaking hands with first one, then the other woman. The blonde held the handshake slightly longer than the brunette.

"You've come to the island before?" said the tall brunette.

"In the 50s; it was different then."

"Less of us?" said the blonde.

"Less of everything," said the man.

•••

The boy stepped into the screened front porch of the sleeping cabin.

"If you'll wait here, I'll light your room."

"This must be a big deal to this kid," said the husband to his wife in a whisper that the boy heard.

The boy placed the lamp on the wooden kitchen table, pumped the tank, checked to see that none of the white gas was spilled. Holding a lit stove match, he adjusted the gas, moved the flame below the mantles. They burst into white light.

"Come on in," he said, moving the lamp to dead-center on the table. Two mantles, half-on, made the small cabin a well-lighted place. There would be no need for the other lamp that sat on the floor next to the curtains of the front window.

Mike barked loudly outside the screened porch.

"Hello the house, anyone in?"

"Just a minute, Mr. Pickett," said the boy. He left the three guests alone in the sleeping cabin and went to greet the maple syrup man.

"Think they'll be interested, Jimmy?" Mr. Pickett wore dark overalls and a red shirt. He looked down at the boy who, at six-foot-three, had to look up at the ramrod-straight man with short, steel-gray hair.

"I think so," said the boy, opening the screen porch door.

"God damn it!" said the husband.

"Daddy! Help!" screamed the girl.

Mr. Pickett was into the cabin before the boy.

There was now more than enough light in the cabin. The lamp on the kitchen table still glowed brightly while the second lamp, the curtains, and the little girl's dress lit up the other end of the sleeping cabin.

•••

"But you haven't been back to the island for quite a while?" said the blonde.

"No," said the man.

"Your wife come with you?"

"No."

"Back home in Brooklyn?"

"Yes."

"Is Brooklyn like it is on TV?" said the brunette.

"You mean noisy, dirty, violent, drug-ridden, generally god-awful?"

"Well, yes. I'd be scared to live there."

"What'll it be, folks?" said the old man's granddaughter. Tall like her grandfather, she wore her jet-black hair pulled back into a bun.

"One gallon," said the man.

"Just one? Are you sure your wife doesn't want more than one?" said the granddaughter, turning to smile at the blonde.

"She's not his wife," said the brunette.

"Are you his wife?"

"No," said the brunette.

"OK. So, mister, how many do you want for you and… your friends?" said the granddaughter to the man, looking past him at the two women.

•••

"Put her on the floor, Jimmy!" said Mr. Pickett, grabbing the lamp, which had fallen on its side and ignited the curtains. The outer edges of the girl's dress were on fire.

The boy had learned Ju-Jitsu back home in the States. He grasped the girl's right shoulder, then used his right foot to sweep her off her feet; she fell hard. He rolled her into the rug. Mr. Pickett went past him, through the screened porch, into the yard, carrying the lamp which, in being dropped by the husband, had sprung its cap, allowing the white gas to interact with the mantles.

Jimmy was still moving the girl back and forth inside the rug when he heard Mr. Pickett's screams.

Leaving the girl, Jimmy went toward the screams, moving through the cabin to the back door.

Opening the door, he stepped into the yard, which was about 50 yards deep before it gave way to the bush.

Mike, not barking, was following Mr. Pickett, who ran in circles, ablaze from head to toe, still holding the lamp, his screams filling the cool, night air.

The catalogue advertised the two-mantle lamp as equal to two 100-watt light bulbs. It said nothing about the wattage output of one lit lamp and one burning man. The human torch lit up the yard all the way to the bush.

Looked at from above, all of this might have appeared to be a nocturnal ritual, a fire dance, man and nature as one.

"Mike! Get Dad!"

The dog headed for the storage cabin.

The boy ran to the all-cedar, big lake boat that rested

on a two-ton trailer next to the sleeping cabin.

From it, he took a canvas tarp. Then he cut across the circle Mr. Pickett was running, tackled the tall man with good form, left shoulder in first, legs pumping, and drove the torch into the ground.

He forced the tarp over Mr. Pickett, wrapped his arms around the bigger man, and rolled with him. Up close he could smell sizzling fat, like meat on a griddle.

Sand hit the back of the boy's head.

"Keep rollin', Jimmy! The sand will help, bring him this way!" said the boy's father, shoveling sand from the horseshoe pits.

Mike paced on the perimeter, fur up, ears up, making no sound.

The husband and his wife came outside the sleeping cabin. They'd taken off the girl's dress. She was wrapped in a blanket. The fire had not made it to her skin.

The boy stopped rolling. He released Mr. Pickett. The boy got to his feet. He had burnt meat on his own hands, most of which he wiped off on his blue jeans.

"I'll get the car," said the father.

The boy pulled Mr. Pickett to the center of the yard. He pulled the tarp away from the face. Two red, smoldering hands covered the middle of the maple syrup man's face.

"You'll have to drive," said the boy to the husband.

"Can't your father drive?"

"No."

"Why not?"

"He just can't."

"What kinda place you runnin' here?"

"You must help them," said the wife.

"I'm stayin' with you and Ann Marie, I'm goin' nowhere," said the husband.

"Forget him, Jimmy, he's not worth it," said the boy's mother, who had come from the cabin with her walker. She had another Golden Retriever with her. The younger dog looked out from behind her skirt.

"You sure?" said Jimmy.

"The husband's done enough for one night," said the mother.

The father backed the Buick Roadmaster to within a yard of what was under the canvas tarp.

The mother had brought a blanket; the father placed it on the back seat. She'd also brought a white beach towel.

The father and his son got Mr. Pickett into the back seat. The tall man was whimpering.

"You can do this, Dad," said the boy.

"Sure I can," said the father.

"Here's the towel," said the mother, handing it to the boy through the back window of the Buick.

The boy crouched on the floor of the back seat. Mr. Pickett wrapped his two, still-hot hands around the boy's left hand. The Roadmaster left the yard. Silver Lake was five miles farther from the hospital at Mindemoya than Walkhouse Bay. It would be a 45-mile trip, at night, with fog rolling in. It would take some time to get to Mindemoya.

"What's the towel for?" said the husband.

"To scream into," said the mother, watching the car pull away.

•••

The man paid for his tin of syrup. The blonde and the

brunette bought one apiece.

The man walked to the end of the counter, stepped around it, came to where the old man was sitting.

The man crouched in front of the old man, who rocked slowly, the chair squeaking when it was pushed backward. The heat in the barn made the man sweat.

"Mr. Pickett, it's Jimmy," said the man.

The old man stared straight ahead. The man knew it was no use to look into those eyes. Long ago, fire had lingered there; the eyes weren't eyes.

"Mr. Pickett, can you hear me? It's Jimmy, I've come back," said the man, louder this time.

"Mr. Pickett," said the man, still louder, reaching for one of the large red, scarred hands resting on the sides of the rocker.

"Jim, it's no use, he can't hear you," said the blonde.

"Why's that?"

"He's deaf, stone deaf. That's what his granddaughter said."

The man tapped the old man's right hand with a finger. The old man smiled, gave a salute with his left hand. The man placed a silver dollar in the old man's hand. The maple syrup man held the coin between his teeth, bit it, and smiled wider, revealing a row of gold caps.

"You'll like my syrup, best there is," said Mr. Pickett, offering his hand.

The man shook the red, scarred hand. He shook it for some time. Slowly, he let go of Mr. Pickett's hand.

He stood up.

"It's hot in here," said the man.

"Very hot," said the blonde.

The two of them left the barn. Ahead of them, the brunette was heading toward her SUV and its AC.

"You had something to say to him?" said the blonde.

"Yes," said the man.

"About what happened to him?"

"Yes."

"Was it important?"

"To whom?"

"To him."

"No, not to him."

The two of them crossed a crushed stone driveway, headed toward the parking lot.

"We'll never eat all of this," said the blonde, holding up her gallon tin of syrup.

"You ever eat fried bread?"

"Fried bread? What's that?"

"You're staying at the Sykes lodge?"

"Yes."

"Tomorrow's Sunday. At brunch, you might look for fried bread on the menu; it'll be under 'Heartstoppers.' You can use some of your syrup then."

"Fried bread doesn't sound like a Brooklyn breakfast."

"It's what they eat in Bensonhurst when there're no cannolis."

"No what?"

"Here's your car," said the man as he stopped by the large SUV. The truck was running with the brunette inside.

"Where do you eat breakfast?" said the blonde.

"Usually, on Sunday, I go to Sykes for fried bread."

"So I'll see you tomorrow, then."

"Kids come with you on this trip?"

"No."

"The husbands, they fish during the morning?"

"Sometimes all day," said the blonde.

"And your friend, Marla, is she an early riser?"

"No," said the blonde, smiling at the man.

"About 8 o'clock?"

"That'd be lovely."

The man shook hands with the blonde. Her hand fit easily inside his; her hand was soft and smooth, and the painted nails looked like they received regular attention. The man let go of the blonde's hand. He walked slowly toward his Camry.

In the barn, the granddaughter tapped in code on her grandfather's hand. She told him about the man and his two women. The old man didn't return her tapped message. He opened and closed his right hand as if to feel again the hand he had just held.

The Hoax

"You ready for another one, professor?" said the bartender, his Belfast accent thick enough to draw attention to itself in Belfast.

"Yes, YES," said the professor, repeating himself to be heard.

It was 9 p.m. Thursday. Mid-autumn in Manhattan. The bar busier than usual for midweek.

"Who're they?" said the professor, wrapping a large left hand around the Black and Tan just placed in front of him.

"Some kind of convention, they're from out west."

"Where out west?"

"Indiana."

"Cowboys," said the professor, smiling, knowing that to a New Yorker anyone west of the Hudson is Roy Rogers.

"Yeah, cowboys," said the bartender, leaving to attend to the tourists, two-deep at the bar.

The professor took one long drink, letting the foam from the Guiness soak into his mustache. He added more smoke to the cloud around him, which provided a barrier of at least a few feet between him and the out-of-towners.

One of the tourists laughed loudly. It was not a New York laugh. It had no metallic undertones. It did not slide out sideways from a twisted mouth. This was a hearty, from-the-belly laugh made by someone who lived outside concrete canyons.

The professor had heard a laugh like that before.

•••

"Good work, Jimmy, nice and quiet," said the father.

"Doin' my best," said the boy, working the oars of a red homemade rowboat.

Behind the boy, at the bow, was a large Golden Retriever; facing the boy, at the stern, was the boy's father; between the father and the son was a live box.

The oars weren't fastened to the oarlocks; they moved back and forth, making difficult a clear strike of the water with an upright blade.

"I picked the right night for this," said the father.

"Yes, you did," said the boy, looking at the shore, trying to see through the darkness to where the Longs' cabin was. Carolyn Long would be asleep, maybe wearing very little, alone in her large bed with the teddy bear pillows.

"Jimmy! You're getting off tack! Pull starboard."

"Sorry," said the boy, pulling on the left oar, moving his mind away from the nocturnal habits of his neighbor.

The rowboat encountered no waves; the lake was dead calm at two hours before dawn.

"We're here," said the father.

The boy stopped rowing, moved to the bow, lowered the anchor carefully; the big Golden helping him by sticking its snout over the gunnel.

"You see it?" said the father.

"I got it," said the boy, grabbing the trout line.

•••

"You from around here?" said the laugher, who'd penetrated the professor's smoke barrier.

"You mean Manhattan?"

"Yeah."

"No, but I work in Brooklyn."

"But you come here a lot, right?" said the laugher. He was short, fat, with thinning red hair; he'd already begun to sweat through the armpits of a blue button-down, short-sleeve shirt.

"Yes, I do. You from out west?"

"Naw, Indiana. Muncie, ever hear of it?"

"No," said the professor, whose parents had graduated from Muncie Central High School.

"What're you drinkin'?"

"A Black and Tan."

"Hey, another one over here for my buddy from Brooklyn," said the laugher.

"Comin' right up," said the bartender.

"Thanks," said the professor, noticing the laugher was looking at someone seated at the table behind him.

•••

"You think this scam is going to work?" said the boy.

"This isn't a scam."

"It isn't?"

"Scams are about money."

"So what's this we're doing?"

"This is a hoax."

"And the hoaxee is?"

"All of them," said the father, using his right hand to sweep at the cabins that ringed Silver Lake.

"Here are the hooks," said the boy, who pulled the trout line into the rowboat.

"OK, take out a whitefish."

"Back up, Mikey," said the boy as he opened the live tank. The dog watched as the boy removed the smaller of the two whitefish.

The boy took the fish, placed a hook in its mouth from the trout line, set it, held the head with his left hand, and ripped out the hook with his right, leaving the mouth on the hook.

"The one that got away," said the boy.

"Fought hisself free after a desperate struggle," said the father, looking at the mouthless whitefish which was supposed to be uncatchable on a hook because of its soft mouth. The father kept his right hand on the seat, his left on the gunnel.

"No, Mikey, this isn't for you," said the boy, putting the fish in the water.

At first light there'd be a breeze, probably from the west, which would put the whitefish belly-up on shore where it would become evidence.

"Here's the keeper," said the boy.

The boy hooked the foot-long fish deep.

"You need help?" said the father, removing his hands from the seat and the gunnel.

The boy could see his father's hands shake.

"It's OK, I got him," said the boy, lowering the trout line until the weight hit bottom. The whitefish was now four hooks from the surface. It'd be easy to see.

"How soon before he's found?" said the boy.

"Not long. The judge checks it every morning."

"You think he'll catch us out?"

"He couldn't catch out a cold."

"Hoaxing isn't an easy job."

"No, it isn't," said the father

The boy and the father had, just yesterday, driven off the island 80 miles to Espanola to buy the two whitefish. "Putting distance between us and the scene of the crime" was how the father had explained the trip.

"He's the one who'll get his picture in the Recorder."

"He's the one," said the father.

"Distinguished American Judge Catches the First Whitefish on Silver Lake."

"And the last," said the father.

"He'll tell this story forever."

"And all of it will be a lie," said the father.

"Six points for our side," said the boy.

"And he will be a liar," said the father.

The boat moved slowly away from the trout line.

"Damn," said the boy.

"What's the matter?" said the father.

"I forgot to remove the price tag from the tail!"

"You what?"

"Just kidding."

The father laughed, the sound spreading over the bay. The father clapped his hand over his mouth, made as if to punch the boy.

The boy rowed. It was nice out on the lake. The boy's mind worked to stay in the present, but the past edged its way in.

•••

The boy listened to the men wearing suits talk about his father.

"Now, Jimmy, you no doubt know why we've called you in here. The situation at the high school is not acceptable. Your father can no longer…."

The boy knew the men. They'd been to his house, they'd eaten his father's food.

"Of course, there will be compensation. We note that your father has accumulated sick leave amounting to…"

The boy wore white pants, a white shirt, white socks, and white sneakers. He held a white paint cap in his hands. He'd been at work painting the toilets in the administrative building when they'd sent for him. He could smell himself; he could see the white paint on his hands; his fingernails were dirty. He used the paint cap to cover his hands.

"Jimmy, these pension applications will have to be signed by your mother. Would you read them over carefully, then…"

The boy thought of the Colt .45 in his car. He could kill these men. They would be easy to kill. There were five of them, two sitting, three standing behind the large mahogany desk. To the left was the door. He would kill the ones closest to the door first. The others would run deeper into the room. There he could...

"Did you hear what I just said, Jimmy?"

"Yes, sir, I did."

"And you'll get her to sign?"

"Yes."

"Today?"

"Yes.

•••

On the lake, it was just him and his father, and Mike. The oars slapped as they hit the water.

•••

"So, I bet there's a lot of action around here," said the laugher.

"Sometimes," said the professor.

"Me and my friends, we're lookin' for some action," said the laugher.

"The Rangers are in town."

"No, no, not that type of action. I'm talkin' about, you know, wine, women and song, and women. Know what I mean?"

"I know what you mean," said the professor, taking a long pull, getting through the Guiness into the Bass.

"Like that looker behind you, and the two with her."

"You mean Rhonda?"

"That her name?"

"That's her name."

"She's got friends, I got friends, maybe you could introduce us?"

"Be glad to," said the professor, turning to where the tall blonde sat with two others at a table.

"Rhonda, here's a man from Muncie, Indiana, who's just dyin' to meet you."

"My my my, send all of him over here, and his friends, too," said Rhonda.

"Thanks," said the laugher, who signaled to two of his fellow cowboys.

The professor drank. Behind him, he heard the laugher's laugh. He checked his watch: 11 p.m. By twelve, the laughter would probably stop, for Rhonda's real name was Ronan. But for now, the professor could drink and listen to the laugh and move his mind away from this dirty city, from the here and the now.

SnakeShaker

The man's ear was six inches from the viola case.

"Hardly a hiss to be heard," he whispered to the jet-black case.

He'd placed it at the far end of the coat check room. Only up close could the series of drilled holes be seen.

His own alliteration reminded him of one of his father's recitations.

As with all his father's poems, the lines were few, but the presentation was long.

"Faro Nell was dealing cards
To four desperate gamblers.
Not a leaf stirred.
Nor horse turd."

It had been some time since the man had heard his father's poems.

The man left the coat check room.

He stepped into the dining room. There was a wait-to-be-seated sign.

The man walked over to the sign. He didn't have to wait long to be seated.

"Yes, sir. Do you have a reservation?"

The man looked down at the short, plump owner of Ridley's, whose hair had been dyed reddish brown by someone who'd probably been working in the dark.

The owner looked up at the man. The man could hear the wheels turning. The man knew the owner but did the owner know the man? That was the question.

"Don't I know you?" said the owner, peering at the man, whose hazel eyes were hidden behind Armani sunglasses.

"No, I don't believe I've had the pleasure. My name is Bubba Hanooz. I do have a reservation."

"So that's how you pronounce it. My wife wasn't sure."

"That's how you pronounce it," said the man.

The owner had not changed much from the promise of his childhood. Then, the owner had answered to the name of 'Round Ronnie Ridley,' and he'd been a short, fat kid with green teeth that no one had much liked.

The man could remember his not much liking round Ronnie.

•••

"Those are wrong," said the mother.

"No, they're not. Look, the tea cup says 'Noritake' and so does this dessert plate," said the boy, holding up the cup and plate for his mother's inspection.

"They're still wrong."

"How so?"

"I'm mixing and matching."

"Why?"

"Are you helping me or are you in charge?"

"What do you want me to do?"

"Put those back in the cupboard," said the mother, letting herself down at a partially set table, placing her walker by her side.

The boy put seven tea cups and seven saucers back into the cupboard.

"Now what?" said the boy.

"See those cups on the very top shelf?"

"Yes."

"Take them down. One by one. Be careful with them."

The boy carefully took down one of the tea cups, turned it over, read the bottom.

"It says 'Prince Albert.'"

"They all say 'Prince Albert.'"

"But they all look different."

"I know."

"You want all of them different?"

"Yes," said the mother.

"Any particular ones?"

"I need six of them. Show them to me one by one."

"How about this one?"

"That'll be fine for Mrs. Vasta."

"Put it by her place?"

"Yes."

The boy put the Prince Albert cup and saucer next to the Noritake dessert plate.

He put them on a table in the middle of the cabin's main room.

"And this one?" he said, taking down another Prince

Albert cup and saucer.

"That's for Mrs. Hall."

The boy added the cup and saucer to the place setting.

He did this three more times. Sometimes, his mother wanted to see several choices before she made her decision. She had an even dozen of the Prince Albert cups.

There was, finally, one each for Mrs. Vasta, Mrs. Hall, Mrs. Norton, Mrs. Toney, and Mrs. Watson.

The boy knew these names. All their husbands were various degrees of 'shots' in the school system where his father had taught. Positive, Comparative, Superlative; Big, Bigger, Biggest.

"What about Mrs. Ridley?"

"Give her a Noritake."

"Why'd you invite her?"

"She'd see the others come. She'd be offended. We can't afford to offend anyone."

The boy finished the settings. He counted them to be sure. Six were coming. He had six settings, plus one, with a Prince Albert cup, for his mother. There were seven in all.

The table looked good. In its middle the boy had put petits fours, each with different frosting and different decorations. The petits fours were uncut. Also on the table were sandwiches of cucumber, watercress, and salmon mousse. The boy had driven to Little Current at the other end of the island to buy the petits fours; it had taken the boy and his mother most of the morning to make the sandwiches.

"It looks good," said the boy.

"It's all right," said the mother.

•••

"This way, Mr. Hanooz," said round Ronnie Ridley's wife, who was tall and slim with long, red hair. The man wondered what she saw in round Ronnie. Maybe her eyes were bad.

The man followed her into the dining room of the lodge, which had been set up for a high tea.

"This is your table. It has a lovely view."

The man knew the reason for the high tea. Fishing on the Manitoulin wasn't what it had been. The lodge had to find something on a Sunday for its guests to do.

"Is this the first season for these teas?"

"No, last summer, in fact, was the first. Ronald and I had wintered in London the season before last. Of course, we had to stay at Brown's. Have you ever been to Brown's?"

"It's in St. James. On Albemarle."

"I take it you've been there?"

"I was in the area after being at J.J. Fox's."

"Oh, well, we thought a high tea would be a lovely idea for a summer Sunday."

Round Ronnie's wife had said 'lovely' twice in twenty seconds. The man had kept count.

"This is a lovely setting," said the man, looking at the table.

"Mikasa," said round Ronnie's red-headed wife.

"But these, these are Prince Albert."

"I like to mix and match."

"Good for you," said the man.

"Here is your menu. I'll send over Dorothy. "

"Lovely," said the man.

It was, in fact, a nice view. The landscaped lawn ran from the lodge down to the water. The lodge was not far from Indian Point Bridge, which had on one side Lake Wolsey and on the other Lake Huron itself. Before, the Ridley Lodge had been on Silver Lake.

Round Ronnie had risen in the world.

Next to the man was a large table. It was set for seven.

•••

"So, I guess we're done," said the boy.

"We're done," said the mother.

"We're ahead of time; it's only half past."

"Why don't you go and check on your father?"

"He's asleep."

"Can't you, for once, just do what you're told?"

The boy headed for the door; the mother used her walker to make her way to her bedroom.

The boy walked toward the storage cabin. It was mid-afternoon, but the temperature would not go above 60 degrees. That was good. The fans in the cabin wouldn't be needed.

The boy let the dogs out of the storage cabin. He didn't look in. His father was asleep inside. He'd seen his father asleep before.

Mike and Wicky were glad to be out of the storage cabin. They started to play blot-out. Mike relieved himself on a birch tree, but saved some; Wicky blotted him out, Mike countered. The dogs went from tree to tree with the same routine. There were many trees in the yard.

"Here, Wicky, fetch," said the boy, throwing a stick.

Wicky looked at him.

The boy fetched the stick.

"Here, Mike, fetch," said the boy, throwing the stick. Mike brought back the stick, sat in front of the boy, held the stick until the boy removed it.

Wicky stared at the two of them.

Last summer, the boy had taught Wicky how to shake a snake to death. The puppy had grabbed a garter snake by the tail and shook it until it came apart. The boy thought this was a good trick. Later in the summer, when his parents had a barbecue for 50 people, Wicky showed off his new trick. He'd come into the midst of the guests shaking the snake he'd caught. Bits of the garter snake had come off as Wicky shook; some of the snakebits ended up on the guests' dinner plates. Afterwards, his father had thought it was funny. His mother had not thought it was funny.

The boy put the dogs back into the storage cabin.

He held the door open; light entered and lit up his father. The face of the boy's father was bloated, yet the father was not overweight. There were dark, nearly purple bruises on the father's arms. The father's face was very red.

The boy shut the door. It was quarter to. The wives of the big shots should be here soon.

•••

"So, Dorothy, has this been a busy day for you?" said the man.

"Not as busy as I'd hoped," said the waitress.

"What happened?"

"That table set for seven next to you, they never showed up."

"Oh, really? Who were they?" asked the man.

"I got the name written down. B-A-C-C-A-L-A-S. I don't really know how to pronounce it."

"So, there are no baccalas here today?" said the man.

"No," said the waitress.

"Would you send over the host when you have a moment," said the man.

"Is somethin' wrong?"

"No, no, you've been a wonderful waitress. I just wanted to make a recommendation for a new pastry," said the man.

"I'll get him. What's the name of the pastry?"

"A muhjdoob," said the man.

"You better write that down for me," said the waitress.

•••

"They're late," said the boy.

"They're not late," said the mother.

"It's quarter past. They're late."

"Nobody who's anybody arrives exactly on time," said the mother.

"I'll go and take a look with my binoculars."

"Fine, do that," said the mother, who was sitting in a chair at the set table. In the background, music came from a record player. It was something by Fred Waring.

Outside, the boy used his Kohl binoculars. He looked at the other end of the lake, where the Ridley Lodge was. He could make out five cars. They seemed to be a Cadillac, a Continental, a Buick, an Oldsmobile, and a Pontiac. There was no Chevrolet that he could see. Big shots didn't drive Chevrolets.

"Jimmy, Jimmy! I got somethin' for you," said a short, fat boy who'd come upon the boy while he was using his binoculars.

"What do you want, Round Ronnie?"

"You're not supposed to call me that," said the short, fat boy, who talked with his lips tight together so it was difficult to get a good glimpse of his green teeth.

"What do you have for me?" said the boy.

"These," said the short, fat boy, handing Jimmy five small, white envelopes.

Jimmy opened each envelope. He read the contents of each envelope. They didn't take long to read.

The styles were similar. One was curt, another concise, the third clipped, number four was brief, and the last one was brusque. All of them were brush-offs. The five wives of the big shots were not coming to tea.

"Where's the one from your mother?"

"She didn't have no envelope. She tol' me to tell you she couldn't make it."

Jimmy looked across the lake at the Ridley Lodge where the five cars were parked.

He turned and with his right foot kicked the front wheel of the short, fat boy's bicycle. The rim for the tire buckled.

"You broke it! You broke my bike!"

"Yes, I did."

"I'm tellin'."

Jimmy grabbed the short, fat boy by the throat, drew him close.

"You do that, Round Ronnie; you tell them, and you make sure you tell the fathers. You tell the fathers I did it and where I am and to go to hell. You tell them all that. You hear me?"

"I hear ya," said round Ronnie Ridley, gasping out the words.

Jimmy released the short, fat boy, who started running. The lodge was on the other side of Silver Lake. Round Ronnie was not much of a runner. It would take him some time to get home.

Jimmy lit a cigarette. He turned and looked at the cabin. Through an open window, he could hear the music of Fred Waring. He'd have to go inside and give his mother the news. The boy drew on his cigarette. He'd finish it, then he'd tell her. There was no hurry. His mother wasn't going anywhere. She was wearing a powder-blue Liberty of London oxford-cloth shirtwaist dress. She had on navy blue flats. She'd have to take all of that off. She would need help in getting it off. The boy drew again on his cigarette.

•••

"So, Mr. Hanooz, did you enjoy our tea?"

"Lovely, Mr. Ridley, lovely."

"And Dorothy said you have a suggestion for our menu?"

"Yes, I do. When you are next in Toronto, go to the Sinbad Bakery and ask them to show you a muhjdoob."

"Yes, thank you, and I believe that Dorothy has the correct spelling."

"Yes, she does," said the man, noticing that round Ronnie was smiling. Out with the green, in with the white. Ronnie had certainly risen in the world, all the way from

Silver Lake to Lake Huron.

In the coat room, the man knelt and felt the hardwood floor. Cold. That was good.

He opened the viola case and let what had been in out. Some of them went toward the ladies' room; others headed toward the dining room.

The man left the lodge.

In the parking lot, at his car, he opened the trunk and placed the viola case inside.

Behind him, at the lodge, he heard what he would characterize as a commotion.

From an ice chest in the trunk, he withdrew a silver flask. The man closed the trunk.

The commotion at the lodge seemed to be increasing.

From his cigar case, he withdrew a Robusto that he'd bought today in Little Current. The cigar had a Brown Band and the initials J.L.P. on it. The cigar had two qualities the man admired in a cigar. It was strong, and it was cheap.

The man toasted the end of the cigar with a single wooden stove match, then lit it, never letting the flame touch the cigar. He took a long draw. He blew a smoke ring. He drank Cognac from the silver flask.

"What's going on up there?" said a young man, pointing toward the Ridley Lodge.

"Snakes," said the man.

"Snakes!" said the young man's young wife.

"Yeah, it's a nice place all right, but what they need is a snakeshaker," said the man.

He got into his car and drove from the Lodge onto Highway 540. He checked his watch. It was quarter after. He had an appointment at Silver Lake, but he wasn't worried about being late.

Only nobodies arrive on time.

Dire Straits

"Wasn't always this easy to get across, was it?" said a short, wiry man, pointing down at the water.

"No," said the tall man walking by his side.

"Musta been a lotta fun. This sheet they give me back there says it used ta take the better part of a day to get over to the other side."

The man recognized the attitude and the accent, the t's becoming d's, the syntax. Bensonhurst, maybe Bay Ridge. He bet himself a cigar on his being right.

The man was one of 50,000 Americans on a hot, sunny Labor Day walking the bridge from St. Ignace to Mackinaw City.

"It sometimes took more than a day," said the man, who wore Armani sunglasses.

"Oh, yeah?"

"Yeah, and it was also about a half day to get across at the Soo."

"The what?"

"Sault St. Marie. You must've come through it on your way here."

"Oh, yeah, right. You from around here?"

"No, I work in Brooklyn."

"Hey, Carmela, here's a guy from back home."

The man decided to collect the cigar bet from himself that evening.

Carmela did not respond to her husband. She was walking ahead of him, carefully, head down, looking through the grates at the waters below. The wind was from the north, about five knots. In her right hand she held the left hand of a plump daughter of maybe seven or eight; her other hand had a white-knuckle grip on a large, black purse.

The man walked with the family from Brooklyn. He'd crossed the Straits before there'd been a bridge.

•••

"Look at that line!" said the father as the boy wheeled the blue and white Buick Roadmaster toward the docks at St. Ignace.

"Doesn't look good," said the boy, maneuvering the Roadmaster with its homemade plywood trailer in tow into a place in one of the fifteen-across rows.

"How long will it be?" said the mother, her voice barely audible from the back seat, where she'd been carsick since they'd left Manitoulin Island. In the backseat with the mother was a large Golden Retriever. In the front, between the father and the son, was another, younger Golden.

"I've seen it worse. I'd say we have a chance to get over

by seven," said the father.

It was noon. The father, the mother, and the son had seven hours to spend in St. Ignace, in a car, with two Golden Retrievers.

"You want feesh?" A bearded man wearing a faded red-plaid, apparently seldom-washed, wool shirt looked into the car on the father's side.

"What kind of fish?" asked the father.

"All kinds. Whitefish, chub, smoked; do it myself. You want to eat, you let Jack Perrault fix you up."

"Anything else to eat?"

"Cold bean sandwiches, all types of pop, plus tea, Red Rose, hot. She cold out here. How about I fix you up?"

The Golden in the back seat had its large furry head over the front seat while the other dog stuck its moist black nose in the direction of the fishman and drooled on the father's arm.

"We better eat outside the car," said the father, who got out of the Roadmaster and opened the back door. The older Golden jumped out of the car and sat in front of the father, who put a leather leash on him. The boy took care of the dog in the front seat, using a chain leash which he attached to a leather collar.

The boy looked at the lake. The fishman was right. It was a cold, gray day. The wind came in hard from the north. It was not a long trip across the Straits, but all the boy could make out of Mackinaw City were the tall white fuel tanks reaching high into the cold air.

•••

"So where you live in Brooklyn?"

"I don't, I just work there."

"Where at?"

"The City College."

"Hey, Carmela! This guy's a professor, he coulda taught your cousin Dominick."

Carmela, a short, but not small, woman, said nothing as she kept on her way, head still down, right hand still grasping the arm of her daughter. Carmela walked with baby steps, as if she were on an ice rink, causing other walkers to detour around her. They were barely at quarter span.

"My wife's never been out west before," said the Brooklyn native, his black hair not moving in the breeze.

"And that's your son," said the man, pointing toward a boy of 12 or 13 in a green JETS #80 T-shirt with CHREBET on the back, baggie khaki shorts, and green sneakers, who was walking ahead of his mother and sister.

"Yeah, that's Carmine. My name's Rich Pinelli, I got a barbershop on 18th Avenue. You ever on your way to the college, you stop in. I'll take care of you."

•••

By 4 p.m. the father and the son had done about all there was to do in the parking lot in St. Ignace.

The boy had eaten three types of smoked fish, plus a cold bean on white bread sandwich, then fudge and caramel corn, all of which he'd washed down with two bottles of Orange Crush. The mother had drunk two cups of Red Rose tea, hot, which had stayed down two minutes the first time, five the second. The father had eaten only the white bread plus four Tums.

The older Golden, called Mike around the house but in the outside world known as Champion Golden Knoll's Shur Shot II, CDX (the champion meaning he was beautiful, the CDX proof of how smart he was), had eaten the three types of smoked fish twice and was now asleep in the back seat with his head in the mother's lap. She also slept. The other dog, Mike's son, Wicky, was two years old. Wicky was not a champion, and he had no initials after his name.

"I have to walk Wicky. He got into one of the bean sandwiches. He doesn't look so good," said the father.

"We'll be here when you get back," said the boy.

The father headed into the sea of cars, making for the beach next to the docks, where Wicky could deposit his cold bean appetizer.

The boy stood by the side of the car, watching his father try to lead Wicky, but the dog went every which way, sniffing the ground and straining against the leash.

"You want some dessert? I got berry pies, all types. My wife, she bake them herself," said the fishman as he appeared at the boy's side.

"No, thanks. I'm full, and my mother's sick," said the boy.

"She sick bad?"

"No, just carsick. She's asleep now."

"Tell you what, you a nice kid, how about I ask the ferrymaster to jump you ahead on account of your mama bein' sick?"

"He can do that?"

"He do what he want, it's his boat. Lots of people they

give him a little somethin' an' he get them right on. You got any ready cash?"

"Ten dollars."

"How about you give me that ten dollar, an' I give you a nice berry pie, and I get you on? How that sound to you?"

The boy saw no problem. His father was walking Wicky; they would be back soon. This had been a long day for his father. There were no bars close to the docks. The sooner they could get over to Mackinaw City and on the road home, the better.

•••

"This longer than the Verrazano?"

"Nothing's longer than the Verrazano," said the man, knowing that no one from Brooklyn likes to hear of anything being bigger, faster, harder, or longer than what was in the borough.

"How bad does the weather get up here?"

"It snows in the winter."

"No, I meant durin' the summer."

"You get three-day blows. The wind comes in from the northwest. Blows all night and all day."

"You know a lot about up here, don't you?"

"Yes."

"You ever been down there durin' one of them, whatta you call 'em, 'blows,'" said the barber from Brooklyn, pointing through the grates at the small whitecaps far below.

"Yes."

•••

The fishman was as good as his word.

"Drive on, son, there're people waiting," said the ferrymaster.

"My father's not here, he's walkin' my dog."

"Make up your mind, on or off; I have a hundred people who want this spot."

The boy drove the big blue and white Roadmaster onto the ferry, dead center, all the way to the front. The fishman had truly given value for the tenspot. The Buick and its trailer would be first off in Mackinaw City.

The ferry eased into the Straits, heading north, running into the wind; it would have to track north-northwest to find the path of least resistance.

"Where's your father?" said the mother, her voice no more than a whisper as she sat up in the back seat, her face frog-belly white. Mike was no longer with her; Mike was in the front seat.

"Back there."

"Back there! What've you done!" said the mother, her voice rising.

"I got a guy to get us on. The ferrymaster said Dad can come on the next boat."

"Later! You fool! You know what shape he's in, he'll go on the toot back there! Where's Wicky!"

"With Dad."

"Oh my God! What've you done!"

"I tried to help, you were sick…"

"You've got to go back and find him."

"How?"

"Ask someone about a boat, ask the captain, just go get your father," said the mother, her voice trailing off as the ferry rolled from side to side. She lay back down on the back seat.

The boy learned that in Mackinaw City he could rent a boat.

"You handle a boat before?" said the captain.

"Yes."

"Don't go straight across, get close to the shore, tack north, slant over, come in south-southeast. One thing to remember—out there in the middle, it's more than 50 fathoms, the water runs fast. Best not to tarry out here."

In Mackinaw City, the boy drove the Buick to the end of the parking lot.

"Take Mike with you," said the mother.

"Why?"

"He stinks of fish, he's making me throw up."

"Why can't I just tie him up outside?"

"He'll bark. Stop arguing, just do what you're told. Haven't you done enough damage for one day?" said the mother, who lay down on the back seat.

The boy took Mike with him. At the docks, he rented a 16-foot Peterborough Fisherman with a 15-horsepower Johnson SeaHorse. The boy did not like the motor. He'd asked for a Mercury.

The wind had not let up. It came in hard from the west. The day was gray and cold. The boy cursed the fishman for getting him into this mess.

The men at the dock watched the boy try to start the engine. The Johnson was different than the Mercury he had back on Silver Lake. He overchoked the engine, it flooded, he had to wait, the boat drifted toward the breakwater. The motor caught, came on fast, catching Mike off guard.

"It's ok, Mike," said the boy.

The big Golden, its ears back, hunkered on the floorboards. The wind hit the portside hard as soon as the boat cleared the harbor. The boy kept close to the shore; he edged the Peterborough into the wind, gave the Seahorse more gas. The boat started to plane. It was good Mike was with him; 100 lbs. of Golden Retriever on the floor toward the stem added some weight to battle the waves.

The wind whipped water into the boy's eyes; his right hand gripped the gunnel, his left was on the throttle. The boat head due north. There was one life preserver in the boat; it was between the boy and the dog.

•••

"My wife thinks this bridge is movin'," said the barber.

"It is moving, it's a suspension bridge," said the man.

Ahead of the barber and the man, the daughter had freed herself from Carmela's grip and moved toward the railing of the bridge.

"No, no. Mommy doesn't want to walk out there. Mommy doesn't feel well. Let's walk here. Here is nice," said Carmela, re-grasping her daughter's hand, her other hand still fastened to her big black purse.

"Don't say nothin' about the bridge movin' to Carmela," said the barber to the man.

•••

The boy pushed the throttle handle away from him, turning the boat slightly starboard. This he did in stages as he began the five-mile trip back to St. Ignace.

The waves slapped the boat, making the cedar creak.

The boy figured he was about halfway across when he saw a boat coming toward him. He wondered who else was foolish enough to be out on such a day.

The other boat was coming dead at the boy's boat. It was a bigger boat, 18 feet, with a steering wheel. The father drove the boat; Wicky was behind the father, leaning over the gunnel, snapping at the waves.

The father circled his hand over his head, then made an Indian chop sign. The boy got it. The boats would turn, the boy would get in behind his father, ride in the wake of the big boat to Mackinaw City.

The boy steered larboard to begin his turn.

"Lie down, Mike, it's OK," said the boy as the big Golden sat up.

The boats were close, 15 feet apart; Wicky saw Mike.

Wicky jumped into the water.

•••

The man and the barber's family were nearing the end of the bridge walk. The barber now held Carmela's black handbag. The other bridge-walkers were some distance ahead of them.

"Jim, that's your name, right? Say, Jim, anybody ever drown down there? You ask me, I think it'd be easy to get yourself into some serious trouble down there."

"There were some accidents when the bridge was being

built, some workers…"

"No, no, I didn't mean that, I meant back in the old days when all there was was boats to get from side to side."

"Some boats capsized, some people drowned."

"Carmela you hear that! Jim here says we're walkin' over people sleepin' with the fishes."

Carmela kept on, at tortoise pace.

"I kid her along to take her mind off the bridge movin'," said the barber.

•••

The waves swept Wicky down the Straits away from the two boats. The boy could see his dog working hard, its golden back moving up and down in the whitecaps.

"Mike, lie down!" said the boy as he reached for the life preserver.

Mike lay down.

The boy's boat had come hard around. He had a better line on Wicky than his father, who had trouble getting the bigger boat turned and headed south.

The boy gained on Wicky, who was rising the front half of his body out of the water, his front paws pumping furiously, as he was hit by one wave and driven into another.

Steering with one hand, the boy got the life preserver on and his blue jeans and gym shoes off. He moved the five-pound anchor toward him. He had to do this right. He had to attach his boat to his father's to save Mike; then he'd have to go in after Wicky. The boy could see the dog, 50 feet ahead of his boat, still fighting the whitecaps.

The boy let the father's boat come alongside. He held

up the anchor so the father could see it. He moved the anchor up and down. The father got it.

The boats were ten feet apart. The boy cut his engine, five feet…four…they hit, the Peterborough Fisherman scraping along the bigger boat. The boy threw the anchor into the stern of his father's boat; he moved quickly to the stem of his own boat, stepping over Mike. The anchor rope held. The Peterborough was now being towed.

The father drew even with Wicky, who was being tossed by the waves. Paws no longer thrashing, the dog moved as if in slow motion.

"Mike, stay!" said the boy. The dog was still lying down in the boat. Mike had earned his CDX; he knew how to stay.

The cold of the water shocked the boy. The waves had 300 feet of deep water to use against him. The life preserver made real swimming difficult. The boy swam the breaststroke toward his dog.

"Wicky! Wicky!"

The boy's voice had no effect on the dog, who seemed to be floating on the waves. Grabbing Wicky by the choke collar, the boy felt the weight. On land, Wicky weighed 90 pounds. The dog was soaked through. Wicky now weighed much more than 90 pounds.

The dog came to and flailed at the boy with his front paws. A toenail cut the boy from his left eye to his left ear.

The boy hooked his right hand under Wicky's right front leg, kept his grip on the choke collar, rolled the dog partly onto him. A wave washed over them. The boy clamped his mouth shut, snorted through his nose to keep his airways clear. Using his left hand, he took one stroke, one scissor kick, then drifted. He couldn't see his father. Lying on his side at the top of a wave, he could just make out the tall white fuel tanks at Mackinaw City. He'd have to swim toward them or else the wind would blow him and Wicky directly south, down 100 miles of open lake.

A motor roared close by. The boy could not see the boats, but he could hear them. Then the Peterborough slammed into him, forcing him to let go of Wicky.

The dog sank. The boy went after him. The life preserver now worked against him like the wind and the water. Ten feet down, he grabbed Wicky at the collar, this time with his left hand, his good hand. The boy was a southpaw. The dog continued to sink. The boy's left hand could not stop his dog from sinking. Wicky was pulling the boy down with him. The boy let go of his dog. The life preserver took the boy to the surface. The water took Wicky down, and down, and down.

•••

They'd reached the end of the bridge walk.

"Jim, why don't you come with us and get somethin' to eat?"

"Is your wife able to eat?"

"No problem. You get her on solid ground, she can eat anythin'."

The man took off his sunglasses, revealing a ridged scar that ran from the corner of his left eye to his left ear.

The man flexed his left hand, stretching the fingers, then forming a fist. This he did again and again.

"Hey, Jim, you ok?"

"I'm fine. Where do you want to eat?"

"There's a place called Scalawag's that my son picked out. Hell of a name. Scalawag's. That OK with you?"

"It'll be fine."

Near the restaurant, Carmela took her purse from the barber. Carmine and the daughter went ahead to get a table. Carmela walked ahead of the two men.

The man and the barber walked side by side.

"You got family, Jim?"

"Yes."

"You come here every year?"

"Yes."

"By yourself?"

"Yes."

"Somethin' happen to you out there, Jim?" said the barber, stopping to look back at the Straits.

"Yes."

"Somethin' bad?"

"I got in over my head."

"But you came out OK, you're here now. You musta took care of yourself."

"That's what I did. I took care of myself."

"Hey, Jim, that's what we all gotta do. We look out for ourselves, everything else falls into place, know what I mean?"

The man put on his sunglasses. He turned his back on the Straits.

"Jim, what kinda food they got in this Scalawag's?" called Carmela.

"Smoked fish. All kinds. Whitefish, chub. They smoke it themselves. They'll fix you up just right," said the man.

Silver Lake

"So, this your first time on the island?" said the real estate agent, who was no taller than five feet, five inches, but weighed no less than 250 pounds and had more than one chin.

"No, I was here a month ago," said the man, looking at the heaped plate the real estate agent was having at. There were several eggs easy over, home-fried potatoes, hash, ham, sausages, fried bread, and toast, one slice lathered with Wagstaff Strawberry Preserve Jam, another with Mrs. Smith's Apricot Marmalade, the last with South Baymouth Apple Butter.

The agent's first plate had been buckwheat pancakes supporting a pond of Pickett's Pride Manitoulin Maple Syrup surrounded by thick strips of bacon that still had on the rind.

The man drank his coffee. It was 11 am. The lodge's dining room was full. A buffet brunch had been set out.

Several tables formed a half-circle at one end of the

pine-paneled dining room. One of the tables was weighed down in its middle with smoked salmon, fish roe, and whitefish and at both ends with Canadian bacon, venison, a bear roast, duck (glazed, generously, with a cherry sauce), partridge, and prairie chicken. There was a cheese table with Colston Bassett Stilton, English Stilchester, aged Mimolette, Munster Gerome, Cambozola Blue, and cheddars: sharp, very sharp, and extra sharp. A pastry table had three types of pies as well as cakes, tarts, Danish, doughnuts, and scones. There was a table for waffles, which shared space with fried bread. At the end of the half-circle of tables was a tall man with a black beard, a high white chef's hat, and a white apron, who stood ready to whip up omelets upon request. Next to him was a short pasty-faced woman with the same high white chef's hat and the same white apron, who carved generous slabs of prime rib.

The man was sure the agent would gather in most of what remained on the tables on his next trip.

"But last month, that was your first time?" said the agent, wiping egg yolk from the corner of his mouth but unaware of the bright yellow deposit he'd made on his red tie.

The man smiled. There were only three reasons to tell a lie: one was self-protection; the other self-promotion; and the last was punishment. The man selected a reason.

"Yes, it was my first time."

"So, how did you come up? Little Current or the ferry?"

"The ferry."

"That Chi-Cheemaun is some boat, eh?"

"It was OK."

"Really up-to-date. Takes no time to get across. Not

like it used to. My old man told me war stories about how long it used to take on the old steamer."

"Maybe there was less reason to be in a hurry."

"How's that?"

"You like the food here?"

"The best in town. I come here a lot."

"Do you, now?" said the man.

The man could smell the coffee, the fried eggs, the toast made from freshly baked bread, the sharp cheddar cheese. Most of all, the odor of the bacon and the maple syrup filled the dining room of the lodge.

It was a Sunday in September, a week after what was known as Labor Day in the States. The lodge was across the bay from the town of Gore Bay. The man had never been in the lodge before.

But he had been on the Manitoulin before.

•••

The boy could smell bacon. Also maple syrup. The odors had made their way from the galley, down the boat's narrow hallway, passing cabins one, two, three, and four. The boy was in cabin five. He was on the top bunk, next to the wall, behind his father, who was asleep and snoring, with one bare foot dangling over the bunk's outer edge. Below was his mother, also asleep, and also snoring.

"First call for breakfast," called the porter, passing by cabin five.

The boy wished the porter would call a bit louder.

His parents were sound sleepers. There would only be four calls for breakfast. The boy worried there would be no bacon and no maple syrup left by the time of the last call.

The boy coughed, then listened. His father snored, and his mother snored. First one, then another, like a chorus.

The boy studied the wall in front of him. It was gleaming white. He touched the wall. It was slick. It must've been repainted each year in dry dock.

It was cold in the cabin. Under the gray, wool blanket, the boy was warm. There was a crisp, starched, white sheet underneath the wool blanket with S.S. Norisle stitched on it. The boy's father was not a small man. The father and son under one blanket and one sheet in one bunk provided plenty of heat.

The boy looked toward the foot of the bunk. To the right of the bunk was the cabin's single window. He could see the sky. Then he saw the lake. There were lots of whitecaps on the lake. The boy saw the sky again. It was a rough crossing. That was good. The seasick usually weren't interested in breakfast.

"Second call for breakfast," called the porter, making his way back toward the galley.

The boy sneezed. He heard his mother stir below him. The boy had hay fever. One reason for this trip was to escape the ragweed of northern Indiana. There was supposed to be no hay fever on Manitoulin Island.

The boy sneezed again. He blew his nose. He blew his nose close to the back of his father's head.

"You ok, Jimmy?" said his mother.

"I'm hungry," said the boy.

"Red, Red," said the mother, reaching up to pull on the large, bare big toe of her husband's bare left foot, which hung over the top bunk to within two feet of her.

"I'm up, I'm up," said the father, coming awake, rolling over into his son.

"I'm hungry, Daddy," said the boy.

"They call for breakfast?" said the father.

"Twice," said the boy.

"You start to sneeze after the first call or the second?" said the mother, who laughed.

"Third call for breakfast," called the porter, passing by the cabin.

"Oh, it's too late, we better wait for lunch," said the father, rolling away from his son. The father started to snore loudly.

"Daddy!"

"He's just kidding you," said the mother, getting out of bed, picking up her overnight bag.

The mother left the cabin.

"Time for our daily ablutions," said the father, jumping down from the top bunk.

The boy put his legs over the edge of the top bunk, lowered himself slowly to within a foot of the floor, let go. The floor was cold beneath his bare feet.

"Me first, then you," said the father, using the sink in the room to wash up.

"Neck and ears?" said the boy.

"Only worry about the parts that show," said the father, washing his face, scrubbing hard, turning his skin a bright red. He slicked back what remained of his thinning red hair.

The boy followed suit. His face also turned red from the scrubbing; his jet-black hair was buzz-cut short.

The father and son got dressed.

The door opened. In came the mother. She'd changed in the large head in the middle of the ship.

"You two ready?" said the mother.

"We're ready, but I'm worried about there being nothin' for the boy to eat," said the father.

"Red, don't tease him."

"There'll be plenty, won't there, Mommy?"

"You can have all you want."

The boy left the cabin with his family. His mother led the way. She adjusted her walk to the back and forth of the ship. The boy had been right: It was a rough crossing. The ship was coming from Tobermory on its way to South Baymouth. The wind came in hard from the west. The captain had to turn and bear into the wind, then work his way north. The 30-mile trip would take a while.

The boy had his hand inside the big hand of his father. The boy could smell the bacon and the maple syrup. He tried to walk faster.

"No need to hurry, Jimmy; there's nothin' left but vegetables," said the father.

"Red!" said the mother.

•••

The man and the real estate agent left the lodge. A husband, a wife, and a boy of maybe ten walked toward them from the parking lot, which was only a matter of a few yards from the lakeshore.

"They still servin'?" asked the husband, who had almost as many chins as the real estate agent.

"Plenty left, the best in town," said the agent.

The boy walked ahead of the husband and wife. The man watched the boy walk into the lodge.

"So you say you have to drive your own car?" said the agent.

"Yes," said the man.

"Easier for me to show you the sights if we're in one car."

"We'll manage," said the man.

"I need to gas up," said the agent.

The man followed the agent into town.

At the gas station, there was an SUV with a two-ton trailer in tow. The 18-foot Starcraft on the trailer was covered with a navy blue tarp. It had rained hard during the night. The tarp sagged in the middle from the weight of the water.

The man watched the gas station attendant stick a rubber hose into the pool of water on the boat's canvas tarp. The attendant sucked on the hose, then laid it over the edge of the boat. The water came out onto the concrete of the station's driveway.

But it was only water that was being siphoned.

Not gasoline.

•••

"That tops us off," said the boy.

"Good," said the father.

The boy had filled the Buick Roadmaster's tank with gasoline. He'd also filled the tank of the 25–horsepower Mercury. He'd also filled the two gas tanks in the 21-foot, all-cedar Barry Boat that rested on a homemade trailer.

"Red, I'm going to the china shop," said the mother.

"We've got plenty of paper cups at home," said the father.

"A man who thinks he's a wit is usually half-right," said the mother.

"You're busted, Dad!" said the boy.

"She got me!" said the father, who laughed.

The mother walked down the street away from the Esso station.

The father, the mother, and the boy had just eaten breakfast at Marv Wood's Restaurant.

"I think she's also goin' there to use the restroom," said the boy.

"Can't blame her for that," said the father.

"Where's this john on your list of most disgusting?" said the boy, glancing at the Men and Women doors on the side of the gas station.

"Number three and rising," said the father.

The boy's father kept lists. Roughest railway crossings. Best hamburgers. Best picnic sites. Worst tourist traps. And gas station restrooms.

"It's pretty bad," said the boy.

"It's a facility what makes a person pine for a privy," said the father.

The boy knew the Esso station restroom would become part of one of his father's jokes. His father liked to tell jokes. His father listened to comedians on the radio. His favorite comedians were Joe "wanna buy a duck" Penner and Dizzy Dean.

"Can Mike drink this water?" asked the boy, pointing to the faucet by the side of the station.

"Best not to, he's had a long trip. Too many changes aren't good for him. We'll wait until we get to the cabin."

The boy looked into the back seat of the Roadmaster. Mike was asleep. The Golden Retriever puppy had arrived in Indiana from Idaho just last week. He'd come by plane. Mike was the pick of the litter. The father was going to make Mike a champion.

The father drove the Roadmaster and its trailer away from the gas pumps. He parked in a lot next to the gas station.

Another car with a boat trailer pulled into the station. Behind that car were two more cars also with trailers. There was only one gas station in town. It was doing a boom business with tourists gassing up before they headed for their summer cabins.

The father left all four windows of the Roadmaster open two inches. It was June. The temperature would only reach 60. But the father was taking no chances. He had plans for Mike.

"What's that guy doin'?" said the boy.

A white four-door Chrysler pulling an 18-foot, all-fiberglass Crosley on a factory trailer was being serviced. The father and the son watched the gas station attendant trying to stick a siphon hose into a tank inside the boat. At his feet was another tank.

"He's put unmixed gas into one of the outboard tanks; he's taking it out," said the father.

"Why doesn't he just mix it in the boat tank?"

"Good point," said the father.

"They're not too swift up here, are they?" said the boy.

"They're all right," said the father.

"You think Mom's gonna come around about the cabins?"

"The cabins weren't bought for her," said the father.

"So why'd you buy a place up here instead of at Lake James back home?"

"This place won't be like this for much longer."

"What's gonna change it up here?" asked the boy.

"See those cars?" said the father, looking over at the line waiting for gas.

"Yes," said the boy.

"Where are they from?"

The boy looked at the license plates.

"Ohio."

"You've been to Ohio."

"I guess there are a lot of 'Lake James' in the world."

"Yes, there are."

"Dad! Look at that!"

The gas station attendant was on the ground, on all fours, gagging. He'd dropped the siphon hose. Gas ran down from the tanks in the boat onto his overalls.

The father ran toward the attendant. The boy was in his father's wake.

The attendant was face down on the concrete driveway of the gas station by the time they reached him.

"What's he done?" asked the boy, listening to the attendant gasp for air. The air smelled of gasoline.

"The line was already full; he sucked on it..."

"He's swallowed gas," said the boy.

"Go to the OPP," said the father.

The boy headed for the building that housed the Ontario Provincial Police.

The father pulled out the siphon hose from the tank in the boat. He connected a garden hose to the faucet at the side of the gas station.

He watered the area around the attendant; he then watered the attendant.

The water didn't bother the attendant. The attendant was no longer gagging.

"They're here, Dad!" said the boy.

The boy and the father stepped aside. They let the police take over.

The father and the son walked over to the Roadmaster. Mike was awake; the Golden was looking out the car window at the action at the gas station.

"He gonna make it?"

"Hard to tell. If he's got gas in his lungs it's…"

"Bad news?"

"Yes."

"This is probably not something I'd see at Lake James," said the boy.

"Probably not," said the father.

"Not too swift," said the boy.

"Not too swift," said the father.

"We probably should keep Mom in the dark about this."

"At midnight."

"With no moon?"

"Moonless."

Mike yipped.

"He needs to go," said the father.

"Maybe I should have him use the john inside."

"Don't do that. We wouldn't want the dog to get the

wrong impression of us," said the father.

The police car pulled away with the gas station attendant in the back seat.

The boy put Mike on a leather lease.

"Why don't you walk him down by the shore?" said the father.

The boy led the dog away. He stopped and looked back at the gas station. The father was walking away from the station to a building on the corner. The boy had never been inside the building, but it knew what it sold. The building was the only place in town where liquor could be purchased.

"Let's go, Mikey," said the boy.

The puppy and the boy headed toward the lakeshore.

•••

"I'm gassed up," said the agent.

"Good," said the man.

"You follow me," said the agent.

"That's the plan," said the man.

"And Silver Lake's the only place you're interested in?"

"That's it."

The man and the agent left Gore Bay.

It took them 40 minutes to get to Silver Lake.

They turned off Highway 540 onto Silver Lake Road. They passed the English country cottage where old Winslow and his wife, Sadie, had lived; they went around the pond where the man and his father had released, at the end of a summer, a snapping turtle they'd found crossing Highway 27 outside Garrett, Indiana, at the beginning of the trip north. The man passed cabins that were now owned by strangers. He slowed coming down the hill to the lake. He could see, through the tall pines by the shore, most of the lake, the sun hitting the whitecaps, the meadows on the far shore. Silver Lake seemed to be the same. Ahead of him, the agent stopped in front of a log cabin camp.

The man watched the agent get out of his blue minivan. The agent made his way toward the man's car. The man waited for the agent to complete the trek.

"You know it would've been easier if we were both in one car," said the agent, wheezing.

"Why have you stopped here?"

"This came on the market just last week."

"Why?"

"Divorce."

"What's the name?"

"O'Connell."

The man got out of his car. The log cabin camp was down the road from where he had lived. His own cabins were now no more than 200 yards away from him.

The man looked at the log cabin. He'd known the people there. They had not been named O'Connell. The cabin had been in many hands since his time on the island. The owners he had known had been teachers like his father. To make some summer money, the owners had rented out the three sleeping cabins behind the main log cabin. Sometimes there would be more demand than the three cabins could handle. The overflow of guests would come down the road to his parents.

•••

"Never turn down ready cash," the father had said.

"So now we're innkeepers," said the mother.

"It'll only be once, maybe twice, a month."

"Easy for you to say. I'm the one who'll have to cook and clean and fetch for strangers."

"I can help out," said the boy.

•••

"This place has a drilled well. 125 feet. No better water anywhere on the island," said the agent.

"That's good," said the man.

But the water in the log cabin camp had not always been good.

•••

"Dad, I need to talk to you," said the boy.

"Can't it wait?" said the father from his seat at the dining table in the log cabin.

"Yes, I'm sure it can wait," said the mother, who gave the boy a look only a mother could give.

The friends of the boy's parents looked at the boy.

"No, it can't wait," said the boy.

"This sounds urgent, I'll be back in a minute," said the father, winking at the owners of the log cabin, then getting up from the table where a considerable breakfast had been put out.

The father followed the son from the dining room through the living room, which had a large stone fireplace at one end. The two of them left the log cabin through a screen door and stepped onto a covered front porch.

"Couldn't this wait? We're their guests. You know how your mother is about table manners," whispered the father.

"Let's get away from the cabin."

The boy led the way away from the log cabin toward the split rail fence next to the dirt road that ran past the camp.

"This should be far enough," said the father.

"You know where they let Beulah loose?" said the boy, pointing to a small white English cottage on a hill about a quarter mile from the camp.

"No," said the father.

"In those woods behind the last sleeping cabin."

"And your point is?"

"I went up there to get milk, and Mr. Cranston had just got done milking Beulah and he let her go. I took the milk and started back. I noticed she was heading into the woods, so I followed her..."

"Why?"

"Hear me out. I just followed her; I was going the same direction, but I was goin' through the woods instead of the field. I was no more than a hundred yards from the sleeping cabins, and it was there that Beulah let loose and did her business. You know where she let loose in?"

"No."

"It was into the stream that runs down through the woods and under the sleeping cabins and comes up right behind the main cabin."

"This is not good."

"So every year when we stop here and spend the night before opening up our..."

"…your mother gets sick and blames it on her still being carsick."

"I told you this was important."

"You were right."

"So now what?"

"Avoid the water."

"What about Mom?"

"Get her to drink a lot of orange juice instead of water."

"We're not gonna tell her?"

"Your mother have a high opinion of up here?"

"No."

"Do you think her knowing that she's drinking cowcrap water is going to improve her opinion?"

"I'll get her to drink the orange juice," said the boy.

•••

The man walked across the road, away from the log cabin camp and down to the sand beach. The dock had been taken up and stored on shore. He stood on the sand beach and looked directly across the bay to where the Longs' cabin was. He remembered how Carolyn Long had looked in her bedroom on her bed at midday in that cabin. In the middle of the bay were his cabins. The man did not look at the middle of the bay.

He heard the agent behind him.

"They still get the itch in here?" said the man, pointing toward the rip-rap that served to stop the water from eroding into the road.

"The what?"

"Anyone ever have trouble swimming in here?"

"No. It's shallow. What could happen to anyone in here?" said the agent.

The man had seen things happen to people in the shallow water.

•••

The boy could hear his parents arguing. They were having at it about the itch.

"So just what are you going to do?" his mother said.

"I'm working on it."

"Working on it! Working on it! Do you hear that little girl crying?"

"I hear her."

"Do you think her parents will ever again rent up here after what happened to her?"

"I told them not to let her swim in the shallow water."

"Can you hear yourself? Do you really think people will go on vacation to a place where their child cannot go into the shallow water?"

The boy listened. The parents kept on at one another. The little girl of one of the guests had come down with the itch. The boy knew all about the itch. It was like having a bout with chiggers. There was some type of bug in the shallow water.

"They've had to tie her hands down," said the mother.

"You know, they can hear you halfway to Silver Water."

"I knew buying this godforsaken place was a mistake. I told you to buy a place on Lake James."

"I know what you told me."

"So what are you going to do about the itch?"

"I'm working on it."

•••

"Nice lake, eh?" said the agent.

"Nice," said the man.

"Good fishin', good swimmin', good boatin'. Three out of three."

The man knew that the fishing on the Manitoulin was not what it once was. He also knew that Jet Skiers had made boating like motorcyle racing. What he didn't know was if swimmers still got the itch.

"Do you know anything about flatworms?"

"Only type of worms I know about is earthworms. Best thing there is for fishin' in my book," said the agent.

•••

"You think this will do the job?" said the boy, rowing the boat.

"It should," said the father, sitting at the stern with two buckets in front of him.

"This legal what we're doing?"

"Probably not."

"Who're you worried about?"

"Mr. Long."

"Is that because he's a nature nut?"

"Yes."

"But he's not all wrong, is he?"

"No, he isn't all wrong. But he's got no sense of proportion. With him it's all or nothing."

"That stuff kill the fish?" said the boy, looking at the blue crystals in the buckets.

"It could, but it's a trade-off. With the wind comin' in, it's not likely to spread."

The father dumped another scoop of Blue Vitriol into the water.

The boy kept the rowboat on a straight line. The boat was cutting across the bay, heading toward the shallows where there were reeds.

"You think you got it figured out?"

"I think so."

"It was either this or kill the ducks, right?"

"The cycle has to be broken. The flatworms live in the ducks, who crap them out, and end up in the snails, who turn them into another bug."

"And anyone who's in the shallow water at the wrong time and the wrong place gets nailed by the bugs?"

"That's right."

"I guess the only other choice would've been to kill the ducks."

"Mr. Long would've noticed that."

"Will he notice the water?" said the boy, looking at the large, purple circles they were making in the bay.

"He's in Meldrum Bay bird-watching," said the father.

"What if someone else notices?"

"Sunspots," said the father.

"Pretty lame," said the boy.

"It's the best I can think of," said the father, dumping more Blue Vitriol into the water.

•••

It had been four decades ago and in another century

that the man had rowed his father across the bay. No fish had ever died. No one had died from eating the fish. And, after that day, no one had got the itch.

•••

"576,241. That's what she be," said the wizened old man, who wore a green cotton shirt, green cotton slacks held up by a black cloth belt, and brown corduroy slippers with white socks.

The boy watched the train disappear down the track.

The old man held up his jar. The people in the small group behind the old man stepped forward, one by one, and dropped quarters into the jar. The boy did not drop in a quarter.

"How does he know?" said the boy.

"He's an idiot savant," said the father.

"Maybe so, but how do we know he's added up all the boxcar numbers correctly?" said the boy.

"Good point," said the father.

The two of them walked away from the tracks. The crowd around the counter dispersed. The next train was not due for two hours. The counter sat, the jar of quarters in his lap, in a green wooden chair. He wasn't going anywhere.

"You look better," said the boy.

"I feel better," said the father.

"I could have you home by nighttime," said the boy.

"No, but thanks," said the father.

"Food ok?"

"The food is fine."

"You safe here?"

"Safer here then out there," said the father, pointing across the grounds to the fence that ringed the asylum.

"So, I'll see you next week," said the boy.

"I'll see you," said the father.

The boy shook his father's hand. The hand seemed smaller. His own hand no longer fit inside it.

The boy walked away. He passed the counter.

"576,244," said the boy.

"What!" said the counter.

"I stopped the train. I counted the boxcar numbers myself. You were off by three," said the boy.

He left the grounds, leaving his father behind.

•••

"So, do you want to see this place?" said the agent.

"Maybe later."

"That's the only place you want to see?" said the agent, pointing to the three cabins in the middle of the bay.

"That's the place."

The man and the agent walked back to their cars.

The man followed the agent to the middle of the bay. He parked his car in front of the main cabin.

The agent was already at the back door.

"It's open," called the agent.

The man walked to the cabin. The door was open. He stepped into the cabin. The present vanished. He was in the past.

•••

"Hallo, hallo, anyone to home? Hallo."

The boy heard the woman at the front door. It was the third time she'd called out. He'd heard her the first and second times.

"Coming," said the boy, walking from the kitchen to the front door of the cabin.

At one time, Mike would've barked to announce that strangers were on the grounds, but now, there was no barking.

"Hallo, Jimmy, can we interest you in some of Betsy's doin's?" said a large woman dressed in man's clothes. Next to her was a small woman with no eyebrows and red, scarred ears, who wore a dirty blue dress and a dirty black cap pulled down tight over her head.

The boy knew the two. Martha Briggs was the name of the large woman; her sister's name was Betsy, but everyone on Silver Lake referred to them as Baldy and the Wee One.

Each summer they worked their way down the rows of cabins on the lake selling the crafts carved by the Wee One.

Years ago, the boy had asked his parents about the Wee One.

"What's the matter with her?" said the boy.

"She's an idiot savant," said the father.

"What does that mean?" asked the boy.

"She can't do normal things, but she can do one thing well. In her case, it's those quill boxes she makes."

"Who were her parents?" asked the boy.

"Wolves," said the mother.

The father and the son looked at one another. The mother was not known for making jokes. The father and the son had laughed.

"Packin' up, Jimmy?" said Baldy Briggs, sitting at the dining room table, using a stove match to light her pipe. She took off her floppy black hat. What remained of her hair hung in greasy locks. The shack where Baldy and the Wee One lived did not have running water. The room took on the odor of the two women. The boy lit a cigarette.

"Yes."

"Sellin' out?"

"Yes," said the boy.

"I hear tell you're gonna be a professor."

"That's right."

"This cabin gonna pay for your schoolin'?"

"Yes."

"You was always a smart boy, Jimmy."

"What do you have for sale?"

"Quillboxes."

That was no surprise to the boy. The Wee One was well known for using birch bark and porcupine quills to make the small boxes. Each box was a different color. The quills themselves were white with a black tip, but the Wee One used dye. The smaller boxes were completely covered with the porcupine quills while the bigger boxes had rough, birch bark coverings. Each box was decorated with the image of an animal.

"I also got some porcupine patties for sale. That big dog ain't around, is he? I got the patties outside in my cart. Wouldn't want him to eat up my profits."

"No, he's not here."

"Dead?"

"Dead."

Even Champions grow old. Mike's back legs had gone

bad on him. The vet had done what he could, but the steroids that reduced the swelling in Mike's joints destroyed his kidneys.

The boy had to carry Mike into a white room.

"You sure this won't hurt him?" said the boy.

"He'll just go to sleep," said the vet.

The boy watched as the vet injected Mike. In the boy's pocket was a Colt .45. At any sign of pain, he would kill Mike. Then he would kill the vet.

Mike's breathing became fainter. The boy petted Mike's head. The breathing stopped.

"He's gone," said the vet.

"You make sure you cremate him all by himself. I don't want him mixed up with other dogs," said the boy.

"Will do," said the vet.

The boy had left Mike, alone and dead, in the white room.

Baldy Briggs looked around the cabin. At one end was a stone fireplace.

On it was a ten-by-three-foot mantle cut from one stone.

"I remember what it took to get that mantle up there," said Baldy.

"It took you and Finney Twist and Homer Cranston and his brother and Larry Lutton and my father," the boy said.

"Your father tol' me I had the strength of two men," said Baldy.

"Yes, he did," said Jimmy.

The Wee One farted.

"Her stomach's been actin' up on her lately," said Baldy.

The boy drew on his cigarette.

"Too bad about your folks," said Baldy.

"Yes, too bad," said the boy.

The boy should've known better than to trust those who'd been put in charge of others.

He'd called the asylum to check up on his father. They'd given the father Antabuse, a drug only for the hard-core. Alcohol and Antabuse won't tolerate one another. One drink sets off hours of vomiting. The father had swallowed one Antabuse pill and been given a daypass into Richmond.

"I see," said the boy, listening to the voice on the phone.

"And he's where now?" said the boy.

"I see," said the boy.

The boy hung up. He had to go to the asylum. His mother was asleep. It would take him five hours to drive to the asylum. He had to make arrangements for his father, who'd waited until the end of the day for the Antabuse to pass out of his system, then gone into a bar in Richmond. In vomiting, he'd ruptured a blood vessel in his throat. He'd drowned on his own blood. The boy did not think the asylum would call his house again. He had called them. They had given him the news. There was no reason for them to call again. He would go to Richmond and get underway with the funeral arrangements. Then he would tell his mother.

It was when he arrived back home, after he'd sent his father off to be cremated, after he'd driven ten hours in one day, that he'd found his mother.

His mother had not been sleeping well. The doctor had given her sleeping pills. The asylum had called the house again. They had not told the boy when he was there packing off the father that they would call the mother. The mother had been alone when she received the news about her husband. The boy had not been there with her.

When he got home, the boy found his mother. The bottle of sleeping pills, now empty, was on the floor by the side of her small bed in the dining room.

He should've known better than to trust those who'd been put in charge of others.

"Your mother killed herself is how I heard it," said Baldy, puffing on her pipe.

The boy looked at Baldy Briggs. Then he turned to face the Wee One.

"Who was it started the fire that burned off your hair?" said the boy.

"It wuz her!" said the Wee One, pointing a dirty finger at Baldy.

The boy turned back to face Baldy. He blew his cigarette smoke her way.

The loudest noise in the main room of the cabin was the raspy breathing of the Wee One.

"How many boxes ya want?" said Baldy.

"How many boxes ya got?" said the boy.

"Five."

"Here's ten dollars, American."

"You want all five?"

"Yeah, I'm low on kindlin'," said the boy.

After Baldy and the Wee One left the cabin, the boy chain-lit a new cigarette. The room still smelled of them.

It was quiet in the cabin. There were two empty jars on the mantle. He'd rowed to the middle of Silver Lake and scattered his father's ashes. His mother he had buried in a silver coffin, under a large gravestone, back at her family home in Indiana. Mike's ashes he had thrown from the new bridge at the Straits down into the water. There'd been a north wind. Wicky was somewhere downwind. If anyone could find Wicky, it was Mike.

•••

"So what do you think?" asked the agent.

"It's OK," said the man, walking toward his car.

"Well, it's pretty rough, but I can get you a good price, as long as you'll buy the place 'As Is.'"

The man stopped by his car.

He looked at the three cabins. Long ago, his father had planted 20 pine trees in a row in front of the cabins. The trees had been cut down.

"No thanks, I'm only interested in the place as it was."

The man got into his car and drove slowly away. The rearview mirror showed the cabins clearly. The man did not look into the rearview mirror.

Made in the USA
Lexington, KY
26 May 2016